"Relax, Sarah," Mick said.

"I'd rather get to the point," Sarah countered.

"Okay. You want to talk to me about a loan. Fine. You did. But first, I want to know more about you, Sarah. You intrigue me."

Intriguing? No way! Sarah had always thought of herself as plain. Certainly not intriguing. What was this man talking about?

"When you walked through the door," he said, "I knew you were more than just a businesswoman." He smiled at her.

Sarah was amazed by how much this simple expression changed him. Though she was still wary of Mick, she felt drawn to him. "If I'm not just a businesswoman, what am I?"

He leaned toward her. "You're a very sexy lady."

A Risky Proposition was a labor of love for **Cassie Miles**. While writing this book, Cassie got to shop and call it research! Though she has never developed the fine skill of haggling over price, she loves to treasure hunt for clothing, jewelry—whatever captures her fancy at garage sales, secondhand stores and flea markets. Cassie lives in Denver with her two daughters, who, like their mother, are also avid bargain hunters.

Books by Cassie Miles

Don't miss any of our special offers. Write to us at the following address for information on our newest releases.

Harlequin Reader Service
P.O. Box 1397, Buffalo, NY 14240
Canadian address: P.O. Box 603,
Fort Erie, Ont. L2A 5X3

A Risky
Proposition
CASSIE MILES

Harlequin Books

TORONTO • NEW YORK • LONDON
AMSTERDAM • PARIS • SYDNEY • HAMBURG
STOCKHOLM • ATHENS • TOKYO • MILAN
MADRID • WARSAW • BUDAPEST • AUCKLAND

Published May 1992

ISBN 0-373-25494-6

A RISKY PROPOSITION

1

SARAH MACNEAL was hot. The sun's rays poured over her like boiling oil. Sweat had begun trickling down her back, and soon her blue silk blouse would be soaked. At least she'd had the sense to leave her suit jacket in the car. She was disgustingly hot.

Denver never used to be like this in June. Usually it was a balmy seventy degrees. So why was it so damn hot? Global warming? Had the ozone layer completely disintegrated? Sarah vowed to donate more freely to environmental research.

And she wasn't just hot, she was also starving, having skipped lunch. This was the day she intended to track down Michael Pennotti and cross him off her list of Things To Do. And this "surprise" meeting with the infuriatingly elusive owner of Penny Wise Secondhand Store promised to be a royal pain.

She marched west on Colfax, passed a tattoo parlor and a deli with a sign in the window, Pasta Special—which sounded delicious. She'd eat later—the next shop on Colfax was Penny Wise.

A silvery bell tinkled as the door closed behind her. *How quaint!* she thought, as she peeled off her sunglasses. She surveyed the floor-to-ceiling clutter of Penny Wise with dismay. Hardly the setting for a business discussion!

The display tables were covered with dusty cut-glass bottles, ashtrays, candlesticks and decanters. An Elvis decanter? She stared at the figure of Elvis Presley with a cork on his head. Beside the tables were freestanding lamps with fringed shades, chairs and bentwood hat racks. On the floor were cardboard boxes filled with more junk. Old magazines, comics, pulp thrillers.

Cautiously, Sarah maneuvered between the tables and the few browsing customers. At least it was cooler as she moved toward the back of the store.

Some of the stuff was quite appealing. She tweaked the tail on a rocking horse and tugged at the knob on an empty gum-ball machine. She came to a complete halt at the sight of a stunning porcelain doll.

Setting down her purse and her briefcase to free her hands, she reached out to smooth the doll's worn velvet gown. Years ago, Grandma MacNeal had given her a doll like this one—lovely and delicate and destined to be forever admired on a shelf. Grandma had also advised her, she recalled with a wry smile, that ladies *always* wore gloves and crooked their fingers when sipping tea. A lady might perspire, but she would never sweat. And she never, ever wore white shoes after Labor Day.

And most importantly, a lady required a husband. Unfortunately, in all her thirty-two years, Sarah had never managed to find one of those. Ergo, she could never really be a lady.

A perfectly tuned piano chord sounded, and Sarah turned. A skinny young woman wearing a tank top and shorts sat at a piano. Her long red hair was tied into a ponytail, and on her left shoulder was a huge tattoo. Sarah was somewhat astonished when she began to play "Greensleeves."

Sarah murmured the words, "Alas, my Love! ye do me wrong/To cast me off discourteously...." She remembered practicing and practicing at the piano for recitals.

Giggles and nervousness and performing the "Moonlight Sonata" before an audience filled with anxious, yet proud parents of budding Van Cliburns. Those had been such wonderful days.

But those times were gone. No more dolls. No more "Greensleeves." The past was . . . past. If she wanted to feel nostalgic she only needed to traipse upstairs to the attic of her house. This was not the time to be nostalgic. She fluffed the doll's faded skirt and returned her to the display.

Sarah headed toward a counter that was crowded with racks of garish costume jewelry. The man who stood beside the fancy brass cash register didn't look as if he belonged in a secondhand store, surrounded by kitsch and chaos. Because he definitely wasn't quaint. Only the full-cut sleeves of his white shirt fit the old-fashioned flair of the shop. And maybe his hair. His black hair was pulled into a ponytail at the nape of his neck. Altogether, rather an odd-looking person to hire as a clerk!

As Sarah approached, she sensed his restlessness. "I'm looking for Michael Pennotti," she said.

"I'm Mick Pennotti."

He was? She'd expected an older man, a dithering old man who was inefficient but . . .

"Do you have a problem?" he asked.

"Of course not, Mr. Pennotti. I'm pleased to meet you." She smiled. "I'm Sarah MacNeal from the Werner Foundation."

He nodded.

"Mr. Pennotti, we have some business to discuss." He still looked blank, so she repeated, "The Werner Foundation. Sarah MacNeal. Surely you remember."

"Not really."

Sarah wondered whether he was really confused or playing dumb. "You don't recall my letters?"

He shrugged. "Would I lie?"

Probably. The full shirt, his swarthy complexion and his ponytail made him look like a pirate. He probably not only lied, but also plundered and pillaged. Well, if he wanted explanations, she'd accommodate him. It certainly beat standing and staring suspiciously at each other.

"Over a month ago," Sarah said, "the Werner Foundation—where I am employed—received a loan application from you. For the development of land east of town."

Mick glanced over his shoulder to the rear of the store where two men were pawing through old record albums. He hadn't liked the look of those guys when they came in, and he didn't like them now. "You know, Sarah, this isn't a real convenient time."

"That application," she continued, "made its way to my desk. In my capacity as executive administrator in Loans, I decided that your project has merit. I made an initial presentation to the board of directors, and they instructed me to follow up."

He seemed distracted. Still, she had come here with a purpose and at the very least she could say her piece— and more! "I've written you three letters, Mr. Pennotti. And I've left several phone messages, which you haven't returned. So I want to settle this matter," she continued. "I see."

Mick turned to focus on her. She certainly was determined. She'd planted her feet firmly and wasn't going to budge until she got his attention.

But right now, he was more concerned about the two men in the back of the store. His experience as a merchant had given him an instinct for spotting shoplifters and troublemakers. He wanted those guys to be gone before he took on Ms. Sarah MacNeal. "How about if you come back in an hour?"

"An hour?" she said, peeved. As far as she could tell, Mick Pennotti wasn't exactly busy. Not counting herself and the girl who was playing the piano, there were only four customers in the store. Plus, Sarah had the distinct impression that if she left and returned in an hour, Mick would be gone. And she wanted to take care of this business today. All she needed was a simple "No, I'm not interested." Then she could close his file.

"I would prefer to wait right here until you are ready to speak with me," she said firmly.

Sarah held her head high as Mick studied her in a frankly assessing manner. She absolutely refused to be put off by this man any longer.

Finally he grinned. "Suit yourself."

He indicated a ladderback chair beside an oak table. On the table was a china plate. And on the plate were cookies. Fat, chocolate-smelling cookies. Her hunger returned. She was dying for one.

"Help yourself," he offered. "Do you want coffee?"

"Yes, please. Sugar, no cream."

With a superhuman exertion of willpower, she managed not to attack the cookies until after Mick had returned with coffee in a mismatched china cup and saucer. Thus served, she pounced and savored the taste of the rich chocolate chips as they melted on her tongue.

If Mick's attitude hadn't been so off-putting, Sarah would have been content to browse, listen to "Greensleeves" and stuff herself with cookies.

The redhead ended her recital. When Mick applauded, her thin shoulders hunched self-consciously. But she nodded an acknowledgement.

"That was real good," he said. "Before you play anything else, could you do me a favor?"

She bounded toward the counter. "Sure, Mick. Anything you say," the girl said in a thin, reedy voice.

"Go into my office." He held out a key ring. "Look in the files and see if you can find any correspondence from the Werner Foundation. Okay?"

"You got it."

"Does she work here?" Sarah asked.

"No. But she's one of my favorite regular customers. Never buys a thing." He watched the girl enter his office and close the door. "I call her Lil because of the lily tattoo on her shoulder."

"Your Lil has unusual taste in music for a young person."

"That's my fault."

Though he was speaking to Sarah, Mick's gaze riveted to the rear of the store. "When Lil first started banging on the pianos, she didn't know how to play. So I found her an instruction book and some sheet music. Those happened to be the only pieces I had in stock."

"Very interesting." Sarah munched on her cookie. "Could we get started now, Mr. Pennotti?"

"Not yet."

He returned to the cash register to ring up the sale of a lava lamp for a woman.

Though Sarah realized that he needed to take care of his customers, there were only three other people in the store now—an elderly lady, a tall pale man dressed entirely in black, like Dracula, and a shorter, bodybuilder type with heavy shoulders. The bell at the entrance announced a new customer. Two new customers: two uniformed Denver policemen.

"Hey, Mick," one of them called out. "I see you still haven't found a barbershop."

"At least I need a barber." Mick ran his hand across his thick black hair. "Unlike some cops I know. Right, Eddie?"

Eddie pulled off his cap to reveal a receding hairline. "I got hair."

"Oh, yeah," Mick teased. "You're a regular Samson."

While they joked, Sarah noticed that the other policeman had moved down the aisles to the back of the store. He approached "Dracula" and the bodybuilder, who were standing close together. "Hey, guys," he said, "I want to talk to you two."

"We're not doing anything," replied the taller man.

"That's right," echoed his partner. "Just looking around. No law against that."

"That's right." The cop's voice wasn't threatening, but Sarah noticed that his hand was on his pistol. "And there's no law against talking to you, either."

This looked like the beginning of a bad situation. Apparently Mick thought so, too. Stepping out from behind the cash register, he asked Eddie, "What the hell is going on?"

"Stay out of the way," said Eddie. "It's no big problem."

Sarah didn't believe the cop. Not for a moment. Something *was* going on, and she didn't want to be in the middle of it. She grabbed her briefcase and her purse. Now what? If she ran toward the door, would they all charge the exit? Might be better to stay put. Quiet. Out of sight.

While the two cops positioned themselves on either side of the other two men and closed in, Mick escorted his only other customer—the elderly woman—toward the office where Lil had gone. Sarah wanted to cry out: *What about me? Isn't anybody going to rescue me?*

But it was smarter to stay quiet. She ducked down beside the table and peeked over the edge.

The police officer was within a yard of the two men. "Let's see some ID, boys."

"Haven't got any," said Dracula. "So, back off."

His bodybuilder partner leaped over a display table and made a break toward the front door.

The two policemen drew their pistols and aimed.

"Hold it."

"Freeze."

The bodybuilder stopped. Dracula pulled a knife.

Sarah gasped. My Lord, what had she gotten herself into?

When Mick returned from his office alone, he calmly strolled toward the confrontation. "Hey, man, cool it. Put down the knife."

"I'm walking out of here," Dracula said. "And nobody is going to stop me."

"You're going nowhere," Eddie countered. "You're under arrest for carrying a concealed weapon."

"This knife?" Dracula held the blade up and gave a mirthless laugh. "It's no weapon. I was bringing this to sell. This is a secondhand store, right?"

"Fine with me," Mick said. He turned to the policemen. "The guy came to sell me a knife. No big deal."

"Keep out of this, Mick."

"I don't want my store torn up." Staring back at Dracula, he held out his hand. "Give it to me. I need to take a look at that merchandise."

After a moment of hesitation, Dracula flipped his knife with chilling accuracy into a wooden tabletop, inches from Mick's left hand. He then raised his hands above his head. "It's cool, man. I'm cool."

His bodybuilder friend had another idea. He squatted down so he was hidden by the waist-high displays, and started to rush toward the exit.

Eddie yelled, "Hey, you! Freeze."

Eddie's pistol swung in Sarah's direction.

"Don't shoot!" She leaped to her feet. Every muscle in her body was tense.

"Get the hell out of the way, lady."

"Just don't shoot me," she shouted.

The heavy man crouched at the end of the aisle where she stood. He was panting, breathing hard, nostrils flared. His hair hung in thin blond strands. His pale eyes leered when he spotted Sarah.

She saw his shoulder muscles bunch. He was preparing to leap at her, knock her down. And hurt her. Maybe even take her hostage.

Instinctively, Sarah tipped over a standing lamp, blocking his path. The bodybuilder tripped on the lamp and fell flat on the floor beside her. When he looked up, Eddie the policeman had a gun trained on him.

"Thanks, miss," Eddie said.

Numbly, Sarah nodded. *Sure thing. No problem. Just another day in the life of an executive administrator.* With trembling fingers she grabbed another cookie and chomped on it. Her shaky knees gave way beneath her and she sat down at the table beside her briefcase.

Meanwhile the police cuffed the two men without further difficulty, and Mick led Lil and the elderly woman customer—both of them wide-eyed and excited—from his office.

As Eddie marched the bodybuilder toward the door, he called out, "Sorry for the hassle, Mick."

"You want to tell me what this was all about?"

"Ask your neighbor at the deli. She called us." The silvery bell tinkled as he was leaving. "And do me a favor, Mick. Get your damn hair cut."

Mick Pennotti took a seat at the table beside Sarah, stretched and yawned. "Sarah MacNeal? I'm free now."

2

SARAH GULPED DOWN her cookie. In delayed reaction, her heart was beating as fast as a jackhammer. How could she be sitting here, sucking on a chocolate chip? Any sane person would be screaming in terror.

"Sarah?" Mick said solicitously.

She placed her hand at her throat and felt her pulse jumping. Was there an etiquette for survivors of life-threatening situations?

"Sarah? Are you all right?"

Her mouth was too cottony to speak, and her mind went blank.

Lil skipped up to them, squeaking excitedly, "What happened? Who were those dudes?"

"I'm not sure," Mick said. "But Virginia at the deli called the cops. I guess she saw those guys come in here and thought they fit the description of a couple of thieves who've been ripping off merchants on Colfax." Again he looked at Sarah. "Are you okay?"

"Yes," she peeped. Mick didn't seem the least bit shaken. "That man had a knife."

"Yeah, he did."

"And you just walked right up to him."

"Well, I didn't want him to use it. And I hate it when the cops get bloodstains on the merchandise."

Either he was the bravest man she'd ever met, or the dumbest. "Will those men be back?"

"Not today." He leaned toward her. "Can I get you some more coffee?"

"Yes, please. And a tranquilizer."

"I would have gotten you out of the way, but when I looked over here and didn't see you, I thought you'd already left. I owe you an apology."

She noticed that although he said he owed her an apology, he didn't actually say he was sorry. When he scooped her cup and saucer from the table and sauntered toward his office, Sarah tried to calm herself. Deep breaths. She clenched her hands together to keep them from shaking.

By the time Mick returned with her coffee and a cup for himself, her teeth had stopped chattering enough to force a smile. "Thank you." Sarcastically she added, "And I accept your apology."

He sat at the table and turned to Lil. "Did you find those letters from the Werner Foundation?"

"Sorry, Mick. There wasn't anything." She smiled. "Is it okay if I play some more music?"

"Go for it."

When Mick leaned back in the chair and helped himself to a cookie, Sarah had the distinct impression that he'd enjoyed the arrest scene. His restlessness was gone, replaced by a casual mood that seemed to indicate that the apprehension of a couple of dangerous criminals was nothing more than an inconvenience in his normal daily routine.

While Lil played "Flow Gently, Sweet Afton," Sarah asked, "Is your shop usually so exciting?"

"Stuff happens." He shrugged. "So? What can I do for you, Sarah?"

Taking a deep breath, she tried to mimic his matter-of-fact-attitude. "Actually, I believe our business is the other way around. There's something I can do for you."

"Explain."

Mick tilted back his chair, folded his arms across his chest and watched her. Though earnest career women usually bored him, there was something interesting about Sarah. He liked the way she took big bites from her cookies.

While she busily explained her organization, he decided that he liked her looks, too. Her complexion was pale, but flushed—from either the heat or the excitement of police activity. Her blunt-cut brown hair was just a little bit messy, as if somebody had been running their fingers through it. She looked like a "nice" girl, he thought. But definitely not prissy.

Of course, her lecture about the Werner Foundation was unnecessary because Mick remembered her letters and her phone messages. Sarah MacNeal. When he'd read that neat signature, he'd visualized a prim gray-haired lady. Not this cookie-eating woman who was sexy in spite of herself. Whose breasts moved enticingly beneath her silk blouse each time she gestured to emphasize the point she was making.

"The Werner Foundation," she concluded, "is well-known for financing projects that will help strengthen the Denver business sector. Plus, we also fund many charity programs, such as the food bank."

"That's real commendable." Mick looked deep into her eyes. There were little gold flecks in the brown.

"Our board consists of some of the most powerful, wealthy and socially concerned people in Denver."

"And what's your connection? Are you my friendly neighborhood philanthropist? Or are you just married to one?"

"Neither. I'm employed by the Werner Foundation. As for my marital status . . ." She glanced down at her ringless left hand. "That's really not your concern."

"Sure, it is. I don't like to do business with somebody I don't understand."

The bell over the door tinkled, and Sarah watched three chic women enter the shop. At the piano, Lil was playing "A Bicycle Built for Two."

"Let's start with an easy question," Mick said. "Exactly what is it that you do for this foundation?"

"I'm an executive administrator in loan processing. My duties include the screening of applications, making recommendations for funding and following up on the progress of ongoing projects."

"An executive administrator."

His tone indicated that he believed that there was nothing more boring in the world than her job.

"I happen to love my work," she informed him briskly. "I like being able to use my training—"

"You're an M.B.A.," he said.

"Yes." Why did he make that sound like an insult?

"What do you do for fun?"

"Fun?"

"When you're not being so dedicated to these worthy projects."

Not only was his tone condescending, but this wasn't the way a preliminary interview should proceed. She was supposed to be the one asking the questions. "I didn't come here to talk about myself."

"And I'll bet you didn't come here to stop a thief, either. But that's what happened. Relax, Sarah."

"I'd rather get to the point."

"Okay. You want to talk to me about a loan. Fine. So much for the Werner Foundation." He dismissed the organization with a snap of his fingers. "But first, I want to know more about you, Sarah. You intrigue me."

Intriguing? No way! Sarah knew she was the sort of nondescript person who could rob a convenience store and escape by virtue of her averageness. She'd always thought of herself as plain, but tasteful. Certainly not intriguing.

"When you walked in the door," he continued, "I thought you were just another career woman, browsing for a secondhand conversation piece. Then I noticed your purse."

It matched her new low-heeled pumps, but the white straw purse had a duck's head and perky tail feathers. "Let me assure you that I didn't choose this purse. It was a birthday gift from my five-year-old nephew, and he insisted I use it."

"And I saw you playing with the porcelain doll."

"I wasn't..." Her cheeks warmed with embarrassment. "I was merely remembering a similar doll. A present from my grandmother. I'm sorry if I disturbed your display, but—"

"Don't apologize. That's what this stuff is here for. Nostalgia. If you wanted a perfect doll, you'd go to the store and buy one. But memories and dreams? They can't be bought."

The bell at the door rang again as another customer entered.

Memories and dreams? What was this man talking about? Sarah's hectic professional and home life didn't allow time for such leisurely pursuits. "I'm no dreamer."

"Sure, you are." He held up his coffee cup. "When you look at this piece of china, what do you see?"

Why on earth would he want her to tell him about a cup? "Is this some kind of secondhand-store Rorschach test?"

"Humor me, Sarah." He rested the rose-sprinkled china cup in the palm of his hand and repeated, "What do you see?"

What did she see? Maybe . . . a sunlit parlor. A gentlewoman pouring her tea. This woman—tragically widowed at an early age—was dressed in black, mourning her young husband who'd been lost at sea.

No point in telling that story to Mick! It was humiliating enough to be caught playing with the doll. "It's just a cup," she said. "A cup with a splatter of roses."

He smiled at her. This was the first real smile Mick had displayed since she entered the store, and Sarah was amazed by how much it transformed him. His gray eyes sparkled. Though she was still wary of Mick, she felt drawn to him.

"You're holding back," he said.

"What?"

"You had a little fantasy about this cup. But you're not going to tell me about it."

"It's only a cup. With roses."

"Have it your way. But reading people is my business, and I'm pretty good at it. I can pick out a shoplifter at a hundred yards. And a dreamer."

"I'm not—"

"Even your little 'splatter of roses' tells me that though you have an M.B.A., you're not just a businesswoman. If you were, you'd have said this cup looked like four dollars but you'd offer me two-fifty." He set the china piece back on its saucer. "At least you noticed the roses."

His analysis annoyed her. "If I'm not a business-woman, what am I?"

"You're thoughtful and a little bit old-fashioned." He leaned across the table. "You're a very sexy lady."

"I am not!"

"Not a lady?"

"Not sexy," she retorted.

Mick knew she was. The high color in her cheeks was a warm promise. And her eyes—there was a world of sensuality in those gold-flecked eyes. He could have told her about the way her body moved.

"I should slap your face," she snapped.

"I don't mean to insult you," he said. "It's the opposite. I'm admiring you. The way you admired that doll."

"There's a difference—I didn't proposition the doll."

"I haven't propositioned you, either. Not yet."

"This conversation is too one-sided. It's my turn to analyze you."

He nodded. "Go ahead."

She studied him. "For one thing, you don't look like a shopkeeper. You look like..." A pirate, she thought. But she didn't want to compliment him by saying that he was too swashbuckling to be tending the counter in a sec-ondhand store.

"You're not as tough as you act," she said. "And your long hair is a childish protest. More appropriate for the sixties than the nineties."

His hair was also shiny clean and luxurious. Neatly pulled back in a ponytail. What would his thick black mane look like pulled free to spread around his neck? Would it feel like silk? Or rough like the mane of a lion?

She laced her fingers together, restraining an urge to touch his hair. What on earth was she thinking of? Mick

Pennotti wasn't her type. Sarah was attracted to conservative men—not pirates.

She set down her coffee cup. "Let's get back to business."

"Do you live alone?"

"No."

He raised an eyebrow. "So, you're not married, but you are living with somebody."

"Yes." In fact, she was sharing her home with her younger brother, Charlie. And her sister, Jenny. And Jenny's two kids.

He rose to his feet. "Excuse me for a moment."

While he went to the cash register to serve a customer, she sat very still, watching him. He wasn't friendly and open with his customers. His attitude was as self-contained as the snug jeans that hugged his butt and emphasized the length of his thighs. Sarah blinked. But her gaze returned to his muscular body. She imagined the hard contours of his chest beneath that flowing white shirt, the strength in his rough, blunt-fingered hands. Sexy? Oh, yes. Mick was a very sexy guy.

His sensuality had an edge of danger. Being involved with him would be risky and . . . challenging.

When he returned to the table, she rattled open her briefcase and placed a yellow legal pad on the table between them. "Your plan, the way I understand it, is to construct warehouses on a tract of land east of town."

"That's right. But I don't know why you're interested."

"I'll ask the questions, if you don't mind. Now, I understand that you already own this land. Correct?"

"Right." His father had bought the land years ago, when it was cheap. And Mick had held on to it. That flat sixty acres with one wooden warehouse were his only inheritance from his father.

"What, exactly, would your warehouses do? The explanation in your loan application wasn't clear."

Mick gave her a long, hard look. Why did she keep talking about applications? He sure as hell hadn't filled out any forms for the Werner Foundation. He didn't want loans.

"Mick?" she prompted. "Distribution facility?"

On the other hand, it wouldn't hurt to explain to Sarah. He kind of enjoyed thinking about his plans, sharing his dreams.

"Distribution is about two things—geography and symmetry." He took the legal pad from her. "On the East Coast and in the South, there are the manufacturers." At the right side of the lined yellow paper, he sketched smokestacks, representing factories. "On the West Coast are a lot of consumers." For them, he drew stick figures to the left of the paper. "The problem is transporting goods from east to west."

"And sometimes vice versa," she put in.

"Sometimes, but not often. In any case, the manufacturers I've spoken to are in the East."

"Please continue."

"Denver is a natural hub for shipping." He drew a circle in the middle of the legal pad. "Here's where the symmetry comes in." He made three straight lines from the smokestacks to the Denver hub. "The manufacturers send railway carloads of merchandise to my warehouses in Denver, then I would—through a computerized ordering system—disperse the goods to the West Coast." Mick drew several lines radiating from the Denver center. Then he named the routes. "Some go to Seattle. Some to Los Angeles. Some to Phoenix."

"Why wouldn't the manufacturer send these goods directly?"

"Time and money. It takes a long time to send goods from Atlanta to Seattle. And if the order is less than a railcar load, it can be expensive to travel that distance by truck."

"So your warehouses would be a middleman."

"Right. A distribution center."

"The part that interests me most is increased employment for Denver," Sarah said. Now that their conversation was finally taking a productive direction, she relaxed. "How many people would you employ?"

"I've got room for ten warehouses. Hell, there's room for twenty. But I'd start with three. Each one would employ twenty to twenty-five people. Mostly unskilled labor for loading and off-loading the merchandise."

"Over fifty new jobs. And our community needs those jobs."

Mick looked down at the sketch on the legal pad. A very pretty picture. And a very costly one.

"Mick? How long would it take to make these warehouses operational?"

"Before or after I rob a bank to finance the whole thing?"

"You don't have to rob a bank," Sarah said with some exasperation. "The Werner Foundation supports your project. If you cooperate, I'm sure a loan can be arranged. At substantially lower than the going interest rates."

"I don't want a loan." He stood and pushed the legal pad across the table toward her. "We've got to straighten this out, Sarah. I don't know how you got the idea that I'm looking for a loan, but it's wrong."

"You filled out an application," she said. "You signed it and sent it to us."

"And I'm telling you that I didn't."

"Mick, I have the document on file in my office."

"Then somebody's playing games with you."

She tilted back in her chair and stared at him. He had to be lying. But why? Why would he go to all the bother of filling out loan papers, then deny it? Maybe he'd changed his mind. "Let me explain something, Mick. In the course of a month, I see over a hundred applications. Of those hundred, there are only about ten that I recommend to the board. Of those ten, they only show interest in four or five."

He said nothing. Only stood there glaring.

"You've already done the hard part," she continued. "Why wouldn't you take a loan? It only makes sense to finance an endeavor of this size and scope with—"

"Using what for collateral?"

"Well, it's obvious. You already own the land."

"That's right. And that's the way it's going to stay. The land belongs to me. It's not collateral, and I won't risk it."

Every trace of Mick's smile vanished. At the same time, the piano music faded.

"That was good," he said to Lil. Then he turned back to Sarah. "I liked you a hell of a lot better when you were playing with the porcelain doll."

The hostility in his voice made her shiver. "Perhaps you don't understand. I want to help."

"I don't need your help. I work alone. The warehouse will get built when I'm ready to do it." His hand made a slashing motion. "End of discussion, Sarah."

"Very well."

She bit her tongue to keep from saying more. If he wanted to be an unreasonable jerk, that was fine with her. There were plenty of people who would be thrilled to receive Werner Foundation loans.

Sarah rose to her feet and gathered up her briefcase, pausing to say goodbye to Lil who had left the piano bench and strolled up to the counter. "You're very good on the piano," Sarah offered. "I hope you'll keep playing."

"Me, too. But maybe I can't." Lil turned toward Mick. Her thin voice whined, "Mick? Are you really going to sell the piano?"

"I had a good offer, Lil." He was as cold with her as he'd been with Sarah. "I have to take it."

"I'll miss having the old thing around here."

Sarah sensed Lil's unhappiness. Though she knew nothing about her, Sarah hated the idea that Lil would lose something that meant so much to her. How could Mick sell the piano? Her frustration with him intensified, and Sarah decided to take matters into her own hands. If Lil needed an instrument, Sarah was capable of providing one.

"I have a piano," she said. "And I wish to sell it. Mick, will you handle it from this store on a consignment basis?"

"Sure. That's my business, isn't it?"

Sarah placed her business card on the table beside the cookies. "I'll be in touch." She smiled at Lil and added, "Your playing was wonderful."

Near the shop exit, she heard a gratifying note of excitement in Lil's thin voice. "A new piano. Isn't that great, Mick! I'll play that one for you, too. To test it."

"Great."

"Someday, I'm going to buy one for myself. When I find the right one."

"It's always hard," he said, "to find exactly the right instrument. To make exactly the right music."

Sarah turned the doorknob and went outside to the street where cars honked loudly and heat rose from the pavement. Inside Mick's shop was another world. It was a world of memories and cookies and dreams and . . .

Scowling in the blazing sunlight, she walked past the deli. Sarah had no desire to meet the woman who'd called the police. Instead, she got into her car and drove to the nearest fast-food drive-through. There was nothing like a hearty dose of cholesterol to remind her of greasy reality.

With a cheeseburger congealing to a hard lump in her belly, she returned to her downtown office. Though her business with Mick hadn't concluded the way she'd expected, Sarah would cross him off her list. She made a note of the date and the fact that he'd refused her offer of a loan and slipped it into his file along with the copies of her unanswered correspondence, his loan application and a memo from Donald Whelan, a member of the Werner Foundation's board of directors, suggesting strongly that Sarah look into this proposed warehouse operation.

She pulled out the loan application form that he claimed never to have sent. It was typed, but there was his signature on the bottom line: "Michael Pennotti."

With an irrational stab of regret, she closed the manila folder. Nowhere in his file was there a reference to his grey eyes, his ponytail or the sudden warmth of his smile. Nowhere did it say that Mick Pennotti was cool in the face of danger.

Her time with him had been intense—from the capture of two criminals to his blatant assertion that she was sexy. But that association was over, and Sarah had to get on with her life. She'd made Mick the offer. He'd refused. Case closed.

She settled down in her office and tackled the business of the afternoon.

First came a follow-up interview with the founders of a ski school. Among their many programs, they offered special classes for children from low-income families. Last winter, the Werner Foundation had provided them with a start-up loan. Their only collateral had been a late-model bus, which they now needed to sell in order to purchase more gas-efficient transportation.

While Sarah analyzed their account, her thoughts kept returning to Mick. Putting up his land for collateral certainly didn't mean that he'd lose it. Why was he so skeptical and suspicious of the loan?

Her second interview was equally discouraging. The young couple who sought financing for a day-care center hadn't prepared their proposal adequately. Before she could consider handing them a check, Sarah needed answers to a list of questions, and more financial documentation.

When the couple left, Sarah was surprised by a visit from Donald Whelan. He strode into her cubicle of an office and closed the door. "Good afternoon, Sarah."

The board members seldom visited the trenches. Generally she only saw Mr. Whelan at fund-raising events and at the monthly board meetings, when she would present her recommended projects in the paneled conference room on the twentieth floor.

After rising from her chair, her first instinct was to tidy up the files on her desk and to hide her goofy-looking

Miss Piggy coffee mug. "I'm terribly sorry about the mess, sir. I didn't expect—"

"Sit down, Sarah. I want a full report on your interview with Pennotti."

"But I haven't had time to prepare. Perhaps tomorrow?"

"No, no. Not a formal presentation. I want your impressions. Talk to me as if I were a friend of yours."

Gossip with Mr. Whelan? That was a tad intimidating. She didn't have many friends who had made millions in the home-construction business during Denver's boom period. Nobody else she knew wore custom-tailored suits and shoes worth more than her entire monthly paycheck.

"He has a ponytail," she blurted. And gray eyes, a dark tan. "His secondhand store, named Penny Wise, is charming."

"Is he interested in a loan?"

"No, sir, he is not."

"That's a shame." Mr. Whelan held a small rubber ball in his hand. While they talked, he squeezed and manipulated it. Isometric exercises? Or the Captain Bligh syndrome? "Did Pennotti say why he didn't want a loan?"

"He doesn't want to use his land as collateral."

"Ridiculous!" Whelan scoffed. "I'm familiar with this property. It's over sixty acres, but worthless. Dry, flat land in the middle of more ugly, flat land. Even if anybody was still building houses, they wouldn't build there."

"I see." She sipped coffee from her Miss Piggy mug. "But if the land is worthless, will it suffice as collateral?"

"Land is land, Sarah. It has value."

"Perhaps we could use only a portion of Mick's property to secure our loan. We could make up the difference by leveraging against the warehouse buildings he constructs and the on-site equipment."

"We need the land," Whelan said firmly. "This isn't a little ten-thousand-dollar loan, Sarah. Pennotti needs significant monies."

"Then, I'm afraid, we can't finance this project."

"Nonetheless, Pennotti interests me."

He gave the ball a particularly vicious squeeze, and Sarah wondered if Whelan's interest was personal. "Why?"

"A great many men who used to work in construction—men who used to work for me—are now unemployed. They could use warehouse jobs. And I hate to see land, any land, lie fallow." He slapped the ball down on her desktop. "Sarah, I want you to convince Pennotti to work with us."

"There's nothing I can do. He refused."

"Tell me this. Do you think I'd have gotten to where I am today if I gave up so easily?"

His question was rhetorical. And patronizing.

"You'll do it, Sarah." He went to the door of her office. "I want a positive report by next week."

Apparently her association with Mick wasn't over after all. He was back on her agenda. Whether she liked it or not, Mick was on her schedule of Things To Do.

She drained the dregs of her coffee from her Miss Piggy mug, picked up the telephone receiver and punched out the number for Penny Wise.

3

SARAH HUNCHED GLOOMILY at her dining-room table after dinner. Mick hadn't bothered to call her back. She'd left three messages. Apparently, Mick Pennotti wasn't interested in anything she had to offer.

Sarah stared at the giant tabletop puzzle of a Wisconsin farm. The hole in the sky was much too large. Only a handful of blue pieces was left, and she didn't see how they could possibly fill in the remaining space. The barn, the silo, the trees and the cows were done. But the pale blue sky? She sipped her cocoa and wedged an amoeba-shaped piece into place. Aha!

She liked puzzle solving, the inevitability of coming up with a solution from a jumble of pieces—unlike the mess with Mick Pennotti. She doubted that situation would ever fit together in a conclusive and satisfying way.

There were so many seemingly unrelated pieces. Lil, the piano player. Mr. Whelan's unusual interest. And all those contradictions about Mick and his situation. And the chocolate-chip cookies. Who baked them? Surely not Mick? And secondhand stores and distribution warehouses.

And what about the loan application? Mick swore he hadn't filled one out. But she had the document in her files.

Why was he so adamant about not using his land for collateral? And why hadn't he called her back? He'd told her she was intriguing and sexy. So why wasn't that enough to get him on the phone, panting? Had he been feeding her a line? Was he turned off by her profession? Her M.B.A.?

Her contemplation was interrupted by the arrival of her sister, Jenny, who crept into the dining room and sat on one of the chairs with her legs drawn up Indian-style. Though Jenny had just completed the strenuous nightly ritual of putting her children, ages three and five, to bed, she was her usual blond, energetic and cute self!

Too energetic, Sarah thought. She wasn't in the mood for a chat.

"Finally, they're asleep," Jenny said. "After three re-tellings of 'Little Red Riding Hood.'"

"Did you ever try reading them something more boring? I can always put myself to sleep by reading Shake-speare."

"Please, Sarah." Jenny's blond ponytail bounced. "The Bard is too bloody for little kids."

"Have you seen some of the cartoons they watch on Saturday mornings? Talk about violent! Then there are those Teenage Mutant Ninja Turtles. And ghosts. And rats with cartoon blood dripping from their fangs."

"I had no idea you were such an expert."

"Little animated heads squished down to little animated toes." Sarah frowned at the puzzle. Maybe she should heft a cartoon sledgehammer and bash the pieces into place. "It's just so irritating when things don't fit together."

"Are you really so upset about a puzzle?"

"Yes. But not this puzzle! There's a very weird situation involving one of the Werner Foundation's Board members and a man named Mick Pennotti."

"Oh. Only a work problem, huh?"

"Only?" Mick had sneered at her job, and now her own sister was dismissing her work problems. "Jeez, doesn't anybody take my career seriously?"

"Of course, I do. But I really don't understand your job."

"If you wanted to, you could. You were always incredibly smart when it came to business and finance."

"But I'd rather hear about this guy. Mick?"

Sarah slammed in another puzzle piece. "The first thing he did was to disarm a thief. Then he asked me to look at a teacup and told me I was sexy. And he has a ponytail."

"He said you were sexy? Maybe you should go out with him, Sarah. You never go out."

"Let's please not rehash that again." Sarah's lack of a social life was old news—a shriveled raisin on the grapevine.

"You're not getting any younger," Jenny reminded. "Pretty soon the old bod will begin to sag."

Her twenty-four-year-old brother, Charlie—who had the body, suntan and blond good looks of a California surfer—appeared in the doorway with a sandwich in his hand. "Are we picking on Sarah's bod?"

"Don't you have some studying to do?" she grumbled.

"A comparative analysis of Jung and Freud." Her brother, a graduate student in psychology, dribbled crumbs across the carpet as he came to the table and sprawled in a chair. "Jung would say your bod was okay—an archetype of 'skinny.' It's your hairstyle that's a turnoff."

"Really?" Sarah muttered.

"Looks too efficient. Repressed."

"He's right," said Jenny. "Too straight and too brown. At least let me give you a perm before you see Mick again."

"I like my hair the way it is, thank you."

"Let's call in an outside opinion," Charlie suggested. He yelled toward the kitchen, "Yo, Tim."

Jenny shushed him. "The kids are asleep."

A huge young man appeared in the doorway. He waved shyly.

"So, Timmy, what do you think of my sister's hair?" Charlie asked.

He shuffled his feet and grinned. "It's nice."

"Thank you, Tim," Sarah said. "Now, may we drop this subject?"

"Sure," Charlie good-naturedly replied. "By the way, Tim's going to be staying with me in the basement for a while. His girlfriend threw him out."

Just what Sarah didn't need was another body in the house—even if he did think her hair was nice. In repressed silence, she cursed the impulse that had caused her, four years ago, to buy this rambling old house from her parents. It would have been far more clever if she, like Mom and Dad, had taken a condo in Miami—a semitropical empty nest.

"It's okay for Tim to stay here, isn't it?" Charlie asked. "I mean, you know how expensive it is to rent, and Tim needs a couple of weeks to get some cash together."

She looked up at gangly Tim and saw a flicker of sadness in his puppy-dog eyes. Broken up with his girl, had he? Oh, well. A couple of weeks wouldn't hurt anything. *"Mí casa es sua casa,"* she said. "But don't clutter the main floor of the house. And I expect a weekly cash contribution toward groceries."

Charlie bounded to his feet and slapped palms in a high five with Tim. "I told you my big sister was cool."

That was her, all right. Cool. And a sucker for anybody with a tale of woe. She watched the two young men disappear into the basement, then slipped another piece into the puzzle.

Her sister grumbled, "Good grief, Sarah! You don't have to take in every stray that shows up on your doorstep."

Apparently the fact that Jenny and her two children were staying here while Richard, her scientist husband, was off on a project in Australia had conveniently slipped her sister's mind.

"You need a life of your own," Jenny said. "Take me, for example. By staying here with you, I'm able to save money toward a down payment on a house of our own."

"That's great, Jen."

"No, it's not. Who am I fooling?"

At the uncharacteristic pessimism in her sister's voice, Sarah glanced up. "Something wrong?"

"Richard sends his paychecks home, but I'm not saving as much as I'd hoped. Even with coupon clipping and shopping at sales. I mean, I'm glad that he has this assignment—even if it means he's gone for six months in Australia. But it's hard." She shook her curls. "I wish I could get a job, but day care for two little kids is so expensive that it's not worth it."

"Maybe you can do something from home?"

"Like what?"

"How about a garage sale?" Sarah suggested. "I know it's not going to make a fortune, but there are decades of family junk in the attic, and I'd be delighted if you'd clear it out."

"Mom and Dad's stuff, too? Do you think they'd mind?"

"I doubt it." Mom and Dad were probably occupied with carefree sunbathing and golfing. Still, she added, "Maybe you should take an inventory and send it to them in Florida."

"You're brilliant! I'll start right now."

"Now? In the middle of the night?"

"It's only nine, Sarah." She dashed from the room and up the front staircase.

With her sister gone, Sarah slipped the last puzzle piece into place. Wisconsin—cows, silo and sky—was beautiful, neat, complete. But what about Mick?

She sighed when she heard the doorbell ring. Maybe it was Tim's girlfriend, wanting to take him back? Ha! Sarah should be so lucky.

She opened the door to the man with a ponytail.

Mick had changed from the flowing pirate blouse to a black Harley-Davidson T-shirt that stretched tightly across his chest. The short sleeves displayed his well-defined biceps.

He wasn't smiling. "Hi, Sarah. I hope it's not too late."

Too late for what? She unlocked the screen door but hesitated before opening it. "How did you know where I live?"

"Your card."

When he held up the small white rectangle, she knew exactly what had happened. In her haste to leave his shop, she'd given him one of her personal cards with business *and* home address. An accident? Charlie would have called it a Freudian slip—proof of an unconscious desire to see Mick. She pushed the screen door wide. "Please come in."

Once again, his clothing made her think of a costume. But this time, there was no hint of the romantic. The black Harley shirt against his tan made him look dangerous and hard—like someone who rode a motorcycle. Not a grungy biker with tattoos, but a rebel who could only be tamed by a woman's touch. And she wanted to touch him. She wanted to glide her fingers over the hard sinews in his arms.

Another fantasy? Sarah groaned inwardly. She couldn't be near this man without creating a fantastic scenario. Given her meeting with Donald Whelan, these fantasies were utterly inappropriate. If ever there was a time to be cool and professional, this was it.

"I don't have my paperwork with me," she said. "But if you've reconsidered my loan offer, I'm sure we can take care of the preliminary steps."

"I haven't changed my mind. I don't want the money."

She looked at him. His gray eyes were warm. Hot. Smoldering. "Then, why did you come here?"

"To see you."

His words struck a chord in her—a vibration that started in the pit of her stomach and radiated outward to sensitize her flesh. The night breeze chilled her bare legs. Without the added height of her pumps, she was at eye level with his chin and his unsmiling lips.

"And your piano," he said.

"My what?"

"I wanted to take a look at your piano and see what kind of truck I'd need to move it."

"The piano, of course."

Sarah had almost forgotten her offer to sell the piano so that Lil would have something to play. She ordered her bare feet to move and jolted clumsily into the living room where she sat on the bench in front of her old but well-polished upright piano. Flipping up the lid, she plinked out a melody on the ivory keys, then winced at the sound. "It's not in tune."

"Do you play?" he asked.

"Not in years. My grandmother bought it for me when I was seven. She said that ladies should know the fine arts, like playing the piano."

He rested his elbow on the top of the upright and looked down at her. "Are you sure you want to sell it?"

"I'm sure. I was never good at the fine arts. I always liked numbers better." She flipped the lid closed. "This piano is just a piece of furniture to me. Lil can bring it to life."

"You're not buying it for Lil," he reminded.

"But she'll be able to play while it's in your store." Sarah intended to ask an outrageous price so the piano would never sell. That way, Lil would always have an instrument at Penny Wise. "You will take it, won't you?"

"Sure, I will." He nodded. "But I'll have to charge you for the pickup."

"Fine."

Irritated by his callous attitude, she rose to her feet and stalked to the center of the living room. "Explain something to me, Mick. You place a high value on dreams. But it doesn't seem to bother you to take the piano away from Lil."

"The piano didn't belong to her. It's for sale."

"But surely you can see how important it is for her to be able to make music."

He hitched his thumbs in the pockets of his snug jeans. "If playing piano is that important to her, she'll find herself another keyboard."

"But don't you want to help her?"

"Like your grandmother helped you?"

"But she didn't." Her grandmother's gift fell into a completely different category. Though Grandma Mac-Neal had the best of motives, she hadn't considered Sarah's wishes. "I didn't want to be a piano player."

"Maybe Lil doesn't, either. You've got to let people decide what's right for themselves."

"But there's nothing wrong with nudging people in a certain direction." Like nudging him toward taking a loan. "If you know that direction is ultimately for the best."

When he stepped away from the piano and approached her, she shivered, but stood her ground.

"Do you know what's best for me?" he asked.

"Perhaps I do."

He was very close to her. "And maybe I know what's best for you, too."

Before she could deny his logic, before she could dart away from him, he caught her left arm above the elbow. Mick held her lightly, and he was pleased that she didn't need much restraint. Ever since this afternoon, he'd been thinking about her soft brown hair, her gold-flecked eyes and the creamy skin at her throat, the fullness of her breasts.

In a hundred ways, Mick knew she wasn't right for him; Sarah would fight him. Just like now, she'd think that she knew what was best for everybody else. But she was a dreamer, too. And he couldn't ignore the way she turned him on.

He looked down into her brown eyes. She wasn't frightened by his nearness. She didn't pull away from him.

"You never smile," she said. "Are you unhappy?"

"Sometimes. And you?"

"Never." Her response was automatic. Sarah was independent. Strong. She could take care of herself and would never admit defeat. And yet, Mick's stern gray eyes compelled her toward honesty. "Sometimes I'm not happy. Sometimes I'm confused. Maybe even a bit scared."

His grasp slipped down her arm in a subtle caress. When their fingers touched, she willed herself not to recoil. Though her sensibility warned her that she might be moving in a direction that she couldn't control, Sarah lifted her hand and matched it against his.

Her pale, slender fingers contrasted with his darker skin. His knuckles were hard. His palm was callused from heavy labor.

"Your fingers aren't much longer than mine," she said. "Do you read palms?"

"Of course not. Do you?"

"Maybe."

He raised the other hand, and she placed her other palm against his, noticing the tendons in his wrist and the shiny black hair on his forearm.

They stood slightly apart, palm to palm. It seemed as though a thin invisible wall stood between them. But when Mick leaned forward and lightly kissed her forehead, that illusion shattered. Sarah knew that he was too close.

"I don't need to be psychic to tell you this," he whispered. "You're the sexiest lady I've ever met."

When he spoke those words, she felt sexy. A sultry languor invaded her body. Her eyelids felt heavy. Her body yearned for him. Logic slipped from her mind. Though she was vaguely aware of the inappropriateness of her actions, her identity as a responsible executive administrator disappeared. Sarah felt like a woman. A woman who wanted this man.

Her hands glided away from his. Lazily, delicately, she caressed the sinister Harley-Davidson logo on the front of his T-shirt and reached up to twine her arms around his neck, touching his ponytail. His hair was thick, luxuriant. With a tug, she pulled him even closer to her. Then she kissed him.

A million sensations flowered in her brain. She felt the heat of his body, his hard sinew. She felt his arms surround her. Smelled his clean scent. Savored the taste of his mouth. The throb of his heart pumping against hers set a new rhythm for her—a fast, uncontrolled tempo. By kissing Mick, she was risking everything she'd worked for. She had to stop—to erase this insane moment.

Yet, when she tried to move away from him, she was caught. Mick kissed hard. His mouth consumed hers. He dragged her body so tightly against him that they were one being. God, he was strong. He took her breath away.

When Sarah turned her head away from him, she was gasping. "We'd better stop."

"Not yet." He kissed her throat. "This is what's best for you. And for me."

He kissed her pierced ear, teased the sensitive lobe by pulling on her hoop earring with his teeth.

An ecstatic moan escaped her lips—but she untangled her arms from his neck. "No."

When she pushed away from him, he released her.

"No," she repeated, as much to convince herself as him.

Purposely, she averted her gaze from him, avoiding the heat in his eyes and his unsmiling lips. Getting involved with Mick was a complication she couldn't afford. She could almost feel Mr. Whelan's piggy little eyes observing her, accusing her of unprofessional behavior. She mustn't be close to Mick. Not while the Werner Foundation business was still pending.

Yet, his body had felt so warm, so good. Sarah knew that if she didn't physically remove herself from his presence, she would be back in his arms. "I'll get coffee," she said. "Cream and sugar?"

"Black."

She led him through the front foyer toward the dining room. Their kiss had been a foolish mistake. She hadn't planned on it, hadn't understood the attraction. It added another piece to the puzzle.

"A puzzle," he said.

"Yes." She halted at the swing kitchen door, which was now closed. A puzzle? Was he reading her mind?

"On the table." He pointed to pastoral Wisconsin.

When she looked down at her puzzle, the cow seemed to wink encouragingly. "I like putting together puzzles."

"But not in real life. You don't like to be confused."

"Exactly."

She fled to the kitchen, braced her arms against the countertop and took deep, gulping breaths. This was all wrong. She was supposed to be talking to him about a loan, calmly and logically. But Sarah was on fire. All she wanted was to be alone with him. To touch him again. To kiss him again.

Coffee, she remembered. Luckily, a nearly full pot was already brewed. Sarah didn't trust her shaking fingers to measure the grounds. His kiss had devastated and excited her. She'd found a startling fulfillment in his arms, almost as if she had always belonged there.

Glancing up at the fluorescent overhead light, she offered a mental prayer: *Please, God, don't let Jenny come*

down from the attic. Keep Charlie and his friend in the
basement. Let me be alone with Mick. Please, God, if you
do this one thing for me, I promise . . .

Charlie bounded up the basement stairs. "Who was at
the door?"

She glared at him. "The wind."

"You're really neurotic tonight, Sarah."

"Yes, I am. Now, go back downstairs."

"Okay. After I get some dessert. We're starving."

She yanked open the freezer unit of the refrigerator and
thrust an entire frozen chocolate cake at her brother.
"Here."

"But this is frozen. What do you want me to do? Thaw
it under my armpit?"

Then Sarah heard the creaking of the front staircase.
She sprinted from the kitchen, hoping to catch Jenny before she burst into the dining room and met Mick.

But Sarah's dash was too late. Jenny—with cobwebs
clinging to her ponytail and a small, ornately framed
picture in her hand—bounced into the dining room from
the opposite door at the same time as Sarah entered from
the kitchen. Charlie bumped Sarah from behind. And
Mick sat at the table, watching.

She sighed. "Mick Pennotti, please meet my sister,
Jenny Jackson, and my brother, Charlie MacNeal."

Mick shook hands with both of them while Sarah ignored the meaningful glances her sister cast in her direction. Though Charlie was tactful enough—and hungry
enough—to retreat to his basement with a half gallon of
butter-pecan ice cream, Jenny clearly intended to stick
around.

"Sarah, why don't you sit?" Jenny suggested. "I'll get
the coffee."

"Fine," Sarah said. "Why not?"

She plunked herself down at the table. Why not invite a troop of marching bands and pink elephants to intrude? Whatever had happened to her privacy?

Mick traced his finger across the surface of her puzzle. "Is this the whole family?"

"Not by a long shot. Jenny's two kids are asleep upstairs. Joey—he's five—was the one who gave me the ducky purse. And Jamie is three. I have one more brother, but he's in California."

"Parents?"

"Florida. They moved into a condo. I bought their house. I had it all to myself for maybe two months, then Charlie moved back here to save money while he's in graduate school. My sister and her kids came three months ago, when Jenny's scientist husband joined an earthquake research project in Australia for six months."

Mick leaned back in his chair and studied her. "When you told me at the store that you lived with somebody, this wasn't what I expected."

"I didn't expect this, either. People just keep coming."

"And you keep taking them in."

Though he wanted to be alone with her, Mick appreciated the demands of family. His own family was large, boisterous and all-consuming in their attentions. He loved the Pennotti clan, but he was very glad that they were living in Phoenix.

Jenny whipped back into the room. She'd dug out the silver coffee service and the best china. Homemade banana bread was neatly sliced and displayed on a Wedgwood plate. She placed the goodies on the table and beamed. "So? How did you two meet?"

"In Mick's secondhand shop," Sarah informed her. "It's called Penny Wise."

"Secondhand?" Jenny leaned across the table. Her expression was earnest. "You know, Mick, I've been considering going into the, um, resale business myself."

"A garage sale?"

"For a start. Just tonight I was in the attic, finding possible sale items. Which reminds me . . ." She grabbed the picture she'd carried into the dining room. "Take a look at this, Mick."

The ornate brass frame held an old-fashioned sepia photograph of a young girl. She wore a pale dress, a hair bow and high buttoned shoes. Her dark hair was as straight as Sarah's, and a lace frock hung from her slim shoulders.

"That's our Grandma MacNeal," Jenny informed him. "Of course, that's a priceless photo but it wouldn't actually be worth much, would it?"

Family history, he reflected, couldn't be bought and sold. It was part of life. The continuity was unbreakable. He could see Sarah in this photo. Her touching vulnerability. And the stubborn challenge in her expression.

He looked back at Jenny. "The frame is valuable. You could sell it for thirty-five or forty."

"Really?"

"I'll tell you what, Jenny. If you want to find out about the business of buying and selling, gather up your stuff and bring it to my flea market on Saturday."

"Flea market?" Jenny questioned. "Where?"

Mick reached into his hip pocket, pulled out his wallet and produced a card with a tiny map.

Sarah intercepted the card before her sister could look at it. "This is the site you plan to use for your warehouse project," she said. "I wasn't aware that there were existing structures on the property."

"A big asphalt parking lot, a wooden warehouse that looks like a barn, and my trailer. But don't even start thinking about loans, Sarah. None of this stuff is worth much as collateral."

"Don't I have to pay?" Jenny asked. "To have a booth at a flea market?"

"The price ranges from ten to two hundred bucks for the space, depending on the square footage and location. But for you, I'll waive the fee."

"Great!" Jenny's eyes sparkled. "I'll be there. Actually, we'll both be there."

"We will?" Sarah questioned.

"I'll need you to keep an eye on the kids."

"And what if I have other plans?"

"Do you?"

Sarah glanced from her sister to Mick and back again. "As it so happens, I'm free on Saturday."

Mick felt a surge of pleasure that almost made him smile. Though he had intended to see Sarah again, the plan for her to be at the flea market made things convenient. "I open the gates at dawn," he said.

"So early," Sarah complained.

"It's the best part of the day." Quiet and still. He loved to watch the sun slide across the flatlands and rise up to the mountain peaks. And he wanted to share that with Sarah.

Compelled to touch Sarah again, he rose to his feet, went over to her and lifted her hand from the tabletop.

Her startled expression excited him. Yet there was no fear behind her eyes. Though he knew Sarah liked to think of herself as a cool professional, Mick was conscious of her sensuality.

When he lifted her hand, she stood and came toward him.

"On Saturday night," he said, "after the market closes, would you join me for dinner? I have a family recipe for spaghetti sauce."

She gently removed her hand from his. For an instant, he feared her refusal.

"I'd like that," she said quietly.

"Good. It's late. I'd better be going."

She followed him to the door. "By the way," she said, "you don't live with anybody, do you?"

"We'll be alone. Three miles from the nearest neighbor." At the doorway, he turned and faced her. "Does that worry you?"

"Should it?"

"Not if you always remember that I have your best interests at heart."

When he leaned toward her, intending to drop a friendly kiss on her cheek, she turned aside. "We'll have business to discuss," she said. "On Saturday night."

"Sure."

Sarah watched him until he stepped beyond the glow of the porch light. Her instincts told her to call him back. To indulge in one more kiss.

Instead, she closed the door. That was the sensible thing to do.

4

SATURDAY MORNING CAME early—earlier than the sunrise on mountain meadows. At four-thirty in the morning, Sarah was wakened by the clomping of little feet. Unlike the typical Saturday, those little feet did not race past her bedroom toward the television set.

She heard the door of her bedroom being opened. There were giggles. The overhead light clicked on. The footsteps came closer and Joey, the five-year-old, bellowed, "Time to get up, Aunt Sarah! Mom says we gotta go. That means you, too."

When Sarah opened her eyes, she was staring into the puppy-dog gaze of Jamie, who, at three years old, was far less aggressive than his brother.

"Hi," he said.

"Coffee," she replied.

Inches away from her face, he yelled to his brother. "She wants coffee." He patted her shoulder. "You sleep now."

"Yeah, sure."

When her nephews charged out the door, Sarah threw off the covers, yanked on a bathrobe and headed for the kitchen where she found Jenny. Fully dressed and beaming, Jenny placed a coffee mug in her hand. "This is going to be such fun. And your hair looks great!"

Sarah pulled a strand of her formerly brown hair around in front of her eyes. Yes, indeed, the faint reddish tint of henna was still there. "If I wash it, this rinse goes away. Right?"

"Eventually." Jenny was busily packing a picnic basket. "If you go to the grocery, we need mayo. And lettuce."

"What do you mean, 'eventually'? You said this would come right out with shampoo." She plunked down at the kitchen table. "I don't want to look like Little Orphan Annie."

"Don't be silly, Sarah. You wouldn't let me give you a perm, and Orphan Annie has curly hair. The red highlights are exotic. Maybe if you use some green eyeshadow..."

"No makeup." Sarah sipped her black coffee. *Come on, caffeine, do your stuff.* "I don't want to look exotic."

Hands on hips, Jenny glared at her. "Fine, Sarah. What do you want?"

Peace and quiet. Privacy. The leisure time to sleep in instead of worrying about the work she needed to catch up on during the weekend. "I'll settle for a shower," she said. "A long shower."

"We're leaving in half an hour."

Mumbling and grumbling, Sarah dragged into the bathroom and stood under the pulsing hot water, hoping to fade the red in her hair to subtle highlights. Then she quickly dressed in wide-legged khaki shorts and a silky red tank top with a short-sleeved cotton jacket layered on top.

Assuming that she stayed all day at the flea market, would this outfit be appropriate for her "date" with Mick? Sarah frowned at her reflection in the full-length mirror. More than likely, khaki shorts meant she was overdressed. Visions of microwaved spaghetti on mismatched plates flashed before her eyes. Not that the food mattered. Her nervousness about tonight's date centered on a more sexual kind of hunger.

During the past day and two nights, she'd tried to rationalize their kiss, to dismiss the unfortunate lapse in her professional manner. But she couldn't forget the feel of his arms holding her tightly, drawing her so powerfully that her instincts overtook her usual self-control.

She couldn't allow that to happen again. Her relationship with Mick was a professional one, and executive administrators did not kiss loan applicants. She'd promised herself that this dinner would be a business appointment. Nothing more.

Yesterday she'd tried to do a bit more research on Mick's career background, but there was precious little to be found. Penny Wise had opened six years ago. After a rocky start-up, the store had been consistently profitable. The same was true with Mick's flea market. Though he had resale licenses, employed over twenty people on a part-time basis and paid his proper taxes, the usual paper trails were nonexistent because Mick had never applied for or received credit. His dealings were strictly cash.

It was an odd method of doing business, she thought. And a precarious one. In case of financial crisis, Mick had no credit rating.

"Sarah!" Jenny yelled.

"I'm coming."

Back in the kitchen, Sarah listened while her sister detailed their plans. Last night, after the stinky mud-pack henna ordeal, she and Jenny had loaded a ton of junk from the attic into Jenny's station wagon, Charlie's Volkswagen bus and Sarah's Toyota sedan.

"My station wagon goes first," Jenny said. "Then Charlie. Then Sarah. In case you get lost, I've made copies of the map. At the market, Charlie and I set up. Sarah keeps an eye on the kids."

Sarah exchanged a weary glance with her younger brother. Both of them regretted the loss of a whole Saturday. But what was the choice? Since childhood, Jenny had been the most vocal of them all, and they'd learned that it was easier to accept her demands than to fight them.

"For a middle child," Charlie said, recalling his psychology training, "you sure are pushy."

"Am not."

"Please," Sarah interrupted. "No rivalry at five in the morning."

By the time they were on their way, the eastern skies were colored with sunrise magenta and gold. In her rearview mirror she saw the mountains, clear and blue with melting snowcaps that filled the streambeds with crystal runoff. Early summer was a beautiful season in the mountains. Sarah remembered family camping trips, wading in rushing waters, the scent of burning pine on a campfire. Then she sighed. Her last visit to the mountains had been a business trip to check out the ski school. She never seemed to have time for pleasure.

After a forty-five-minute drive, they arrived. Though the Penny Wise Flea Market was just off Interstate 70, there was nothing else around. Mr. Whelan had been correct when he'd told Sarah that this was flat land in the middle of more flat, arid land.

She pulled into a line of cars that was being checked through the gates by Mick and a ticket taker. As Mick leaned down to each driver's window and consulted a checklist, she noticed that he didn't waste motion. Nor did he smile.

As an executive administrator for the foundation that might make him a loan, she should have been pleased by his attitude of efficiency. She should have been thinking of profit margins, calculating the number of merchants who would rent space, versus the cost-per-foot expenditure.

Instead, she concentrated on the man. Early-morning sunshine glistened on his thick black hair and highlighted the planes of his face. Beneath his light windbreaker, she saw his flat torso. Was she the only one who noticed that he was extraordinarily handsome?

When she came to the gate, he gave one of his rare smiles. "Hey, Sarah."

"Hey, yourself." At the sound of his voice, she felt warm.

"After you've unloaded, take your car around in back and park by my trailer."

He slapped the side of her car, dismissing her, and Sarah followed her brother's van to an unloading area.

Jenny's designated spot was outdoors under a long pavilion of red-and-white striped tents. While Jenny fussed over the displays, Sarah took her two nephews to prowl the grounds. There was a carnival atmosphere as a wide variety of people arranged their booths, and the two boys caught the excitement.

They dragged her toward a large booth that featured a row of Batman T-shirts which were marked down to two dollars each. Joey pointed. "Good old Batman. Remember him, Aunt Sarah?"

How amazing! Even a five-year-old could be nostalgic. "How about something to eat?"

"Popcorn and a hot dog."

"At seven o'clock in the morning?" Sarah cringed. "Let's get some orange juice, okay?"

They located a vendor, and Sarah bought a cup of coffee for herself and orange juice for the boys. Though she would have preferred to sit down and relax, the boys wanted to explore the warehouse.

Inside the vast, wood-frame building with concrete floors, Sarah noticed that the displays were set up more professionally and efficiently. She assumed that these were vendors who sold at flea markets to earn a living.

In a far corner were the craftsmen—potters, weavers and macramé artisans. She sighted Mick, engaged in a discussion with a woman dressed like a gypsy, who was hanging stained-glass ornaments from a slender wire.

Sarah waved. "Mick!"

When he turned to scan the milling crowd, he seemed preoccupied and she had second thoughts about calling him away from his work. Then he noticed her, smiled broadly, and Sarah felt gratified. He came toward her and the boys with long strides.

When she introduced him to her nephews, he squatted down to talk to them. "Jamie and Joey," he said solemnly. "What's your favorite thing?"

"Rabbits," Jamie quickly said.

"Do you mean cartoon rabbits?" Sarah asked. "Or stuffed-animal rabbits?"

"Real bunny rabbits. I saw some here. Can I get one?"

Jamie could be so adorable with his pudgy arms and legs and huge brown eyes, but still Sarah drew the line at bringing livestock into her home. "No rabbits, Jamie. Sorry."

Mick turned to Joey, "How about you? What kind of stuff do you like?"

"I don't know."

"It's okay to think about it," Mick said. "You want to go out to the playground?"

"I don't know."

Joey's reticence worried Sarah. Last year in his kindergarten, Joey had taken to heart—too seriously—his teacher's warnings not to talk to strangers.

Mick rose to his feet. "Let's go take a look at the playground, Joey. It's new this year, and maybe you can tell me how to make it better."

Behind the warehouse, he led them to a large area enclosed with a chain-link fence. Inside were sandboxes, wooden swing sets, slides, picnic tables and a shaded pavilion. The sign at the gate read Supervised Child Care, One Dollar An Hour. There were four other children inside, and the supervisor on duty was Lil.

As soon as Mick swung open the gate, Jamie rushed toward the largest swing set that included a framework of wooden beams for climbing, and tire swings and a bridge. Joey held back.

"What do you think?" Mick asked Joey.

"It's okay."

"I agree," Sarah said. "Is this a concession?"

"Not a money-maker," Mick said. "It's more for convenience. With everything else going on, it's hard for parents to keep track of their children."

"Is Lil paid for working here?" Sarah asked.

"You bet. She gets sixty percent of the take." He gave Sarah a cool look. "You'll be happy to know that Lil wants to buy an electronic keyboard synthesizer. She's doing this to earn some money."

As she followed him into the playground, Sarah revised her opinion of Mick Pennotti. It was a wise decision to provide Lil with the opportunity to earn her own money and purchase her own instrument. Sarah had to admit that his solution was far better than her gesture of giving up her own piano.

"What did you do to your hair?" Lil asked in greeting.

"It'll wash out," Sarah said. "Eventually."

Sarah watched Jamie immediately make friends with some of the other children and toddle happily after them. In contrast, Joey stood alone at the top of the wooden playhouse and swing set. His eyes had a faraway look, and when Sarah called to him, her voice took a couple of minutes to register. Then he climbed down and came to her.

"Joey, do you want to stay here for a while?" Sarah asked.

His lower lip stuck out. "Okay, but not all day."

"All right. You do as this lady says."

She pulled a couple of dollars from her purse and handed them to Lil. "How about if I leave the kids here for an hour?"

"Sure." First Lil pocketed the money. Then she went to a picnic table, picked up a clipboard and returned. She took down the boys' names and the time that Sarah would be back to pick them up. Then she asked, "Are they yours?"

"I'm their aunt."

"You're not married?"

"Nope."

"Too bad." Lil set down her clipboard and stalked toward a little girl on a tire swing. She seemed hostile. But why? Had Sarah done something to offend her?

Mick touched her elbow. "I need to go. This is a busy time for me."

"Thanks for showing me the playground."

"No problem. If I don't see you before then, our date is tonight after closing."

Now was her chance to say no. If she really couldn't trust herself to be near him, now was the time to decide. She blurted, "I'll be there."

"Good." He repeated his earlier instruction. "Did you park your car by my trailer?"

"I couldn't find it."

He pointed east toward a clump of cottonwoods that stood a short distance from the warehouse. The flat roof of a trailer was visible among the trees. Their leaves made a lush contrast to the flat, scrubby landscape that extended for miles toward Nebraska.

When she turned back toward Mick, she saw the distant outline of Denver's skyline to the west. Beyond Denver loomed the front range of the Rockies. Huge and impressive, the mountains dwarfed both city and plain. "It's beautiful out here."

"Yeah. But it can be rough. There are no mountains to stop the force of the wind or the snow. Storms can be brutal."

"And it's a bit remote from Denver," she added.

"A long commute," he agreed. "But we're right off the highway. This is a great site for warehouses."

"Is there good water out here?"

"Let me put it this way—my well has never run dry."

His unsmiling expression made her wonder if his wry innuendo was intentional. When she looked up to study him, Mick leaned toward her and kissed her cheek.

Before she could react, Mick pivoted and hurried back toward the flea-market warehouse. That kiss had been so quick and so casual that she wasn't even sure it had happened.

When she turned and saw Lil's stormy expression, the reason for Lil's hostility became obvious to Sarah. She had a crush on Mick and didn't want Sarah to move in on her man.

Hoping she could clear the air, Sarah headed across the playground and stood beside the girl. "Is Lil your real name?"

"It'll do."

Bracing herself, Sarah said, "I want you to know that there's nothing between Mick and me except business."

"Oh, sure."

"I mean it."

Perhaps, Sarah worried, Lil's reaction wasn't due to an infatuation. In this day and age, it was entirely possible that thirty-something Mick was actually involved with Lil. "Do you and Mick have a relationship?"

To Sarah's relief, Lil said, "We're friends."

"But you like him a lot, don't you?"

"Who wouldn't? He's really great. He's smart and gentle. And he doesn't treat me like a baby."

"How old are you?"

"Sixteen. Not a little girl. Lots of women get pregnant when they're sixteen."

Sarah was beginning to feel as if she was in over her head.

"But don't worry," Lil said. "Anyway, that's not how I feel about Mick."

"How *do* you feel about him?"

"Maybe like he's a big brother. We're a lot alike."

"How so?"

Lil thought for a moment, then said, "He knows what it's like to be alone. To lose everything."

Sarah stood quietly and listened.

"Mick tells me everything," Lil said. "He told me that the worst thing that ever happened to him was about ten years ago. His family lost all their money. Mick was in college and he had to drop out to help out, but it was too late. All that was left of everything they owned was this land right here, and I guess that was because they couldn't find anybody to buy it."

"What business was his family in?"

"Building houses. And it wasn't their fault they went broke, either. Mick says his father got cheated by his partner."

Ten years ago, several Denver construction firms had run into difficulties when the housing boom slowed to a snail's pace.

"And that's another way that me and Mick are alike," Lil said. "After this partner screwed his father, Mick said he'd never trust anybody again. I'm like that, too. It's better to be on your own. Alone."

"Have you lost everything, too?"

"Kind of."

"Your parents?"

"They're divorced. But that's none of your business."

Sarah backed off. "I guess not."

Two little girls on the swing set started a shouting match, and Lil went over to them. When she'd rescued the smaller girl, she glanced over her shoulder at Sarah. "I'm busy here."

"Fine, and you're doing a good job. If you ever want to talk, Lil, I'd be happy to listen." Sarah headed for the gate. "I'll be back for the boys in forty-five minutes."

With a goodbye wave to her nephews, she left the playground. Though she hadn't planned to pump Lil for explanations of Mick's behavior, her story about his family had given her something to think about. His family money problems might explain his reluctance about taking a loan.

Sarah promised herself that later today, she'd find time to think things over. But right now, she had to help Jenny, and she hurried toward the outdoor area where her sister was arranging clothing on a rack and some weird objects on the metal shelves she'd taken from Sarah's garage. Trays and trinkets and teapots. Books and record albums. On the ground were cardboard boxes filled with family castoffs, including two sets of ugly brown dishes that nobody wanted, a couple of lamps, umbrella stands, a rocking chair.

"Your timing couldn't be better," Jenny said dryly. "We're almost done."

Sarah stood before the pièce de résistance—a genuine Tiffany stained-glass lamp. "You're not selling this, are you?"

"Don't worry," Jenny confided. "I priced it at eight hundred dollars. Nobody is going to buy it."

"Then why did you bring it along?"

"Salesmanship. When people see the lamp, they'll assume there may be other antiques in my junk."

"Very clever," Sarah said. "Have you done this before?"

"No, but I've been to dozens of flea markets."

"How does this one stack up?"

"Very well. It's clean and organized, with lots of space. Your friend Mick has done a good job with this place. By the way, what did you do with my children?"

"There's a supervised playground area in back. Do you want me to show you where?"

"Not until after my first sale." Jenny pointed toward the entrance where a long row of cars had lined up, bumper to bumper. "It's almost time. The buyers are coming."

Buying and selling, Sarah thought. Giving and taking. This promised to be some day—in more ways than one.

5

AT MIDAFTERNOON, the skies clouded over, providing relief from the heat but worry among the merchants in the outdoor booths, who glanced frequently at the clouds and shook their heads. Only the farmers with their bright displays of fresh tomatoes and peppers and early corn were cheering for rain. The others were glum. Even the shoppers seemed pushed, less likely to browse.

Jenny, on the other hand, was still as bubbly as ever. Excitedly she confided to Sarah and Charlie: "I've made three hundred dollars—in one day! Do you know how long it would take me to save this much money?"

"Congratulations." Sarah took a look at her sister's severely depleted merchandise. "Too bad you can't do this every weekend."

"But I can. That's the beauty of it. I've been talking to people around here, and it's all a matter of buying and selling. At the end of the day, I'll buy cheap from other people. Next weekend, I sell. I can turn this three hundred into nine."

"Sounds risky to me."

"Not to me," Charlie said. "Jen is a great shopper. Remember Christmas shopping when we were kids? We'd all start out with the same money, but Jenny always came back with twice as much as you or me, Sarah."

"Charlie's right. You've always known how to get value for a dollar. Just be sure you don't deplete your cash reserves beyond the initial three-hundred-dollar profit."

"Oh, Sarah, you're so conservative. This isn't the kind of finance you work with. This is instinct." Jenny giggled. "Who would have thought I could make money from shopping?"

Joey sidled up beside his mother. "How much longer do we have to stay?"

"Not long, honey. A couple of hours."

He groaned. "I want to go home."

"Me, too," piped up Jamie. "I hate the outdoors potty."

Jenny looked to her brother and sister. "Help."

"I've got an idea," Charlie said. "Let's eat."

Charlie and Sarah took the two restless boys and went in search of food. There was all kinds—from spicy Mexican to home-baked muffins. While Charlie selected an esophagus-burning tamale and the boys picked out hamburgers, Sarah opted for lemonade and a cookie. They sat down outside the warehouse beneath an overhang and munched.

"Aunt Sarah?" Jamie said between bites. "I still want a bunny rabbit."

Sarah looked questioningly at him. "What's all this rabbit stuff about, anyway? I haven't seen anybody selling rabbits."

"Out there." Jamie pointed to the fields beyond the warehouse grounds. "I saw them."

"Those are wild rabbits," she explained. "That's their home. You wouldn't want to take them away from their home, would you?"

"Yes."

"Why don't you look for something else," she suggested. "But first we need to clean up our mess here and put it in the trash can."

While the boys gathered burrito wrappers and paper cups, Charlie said, "I expected today to be a giant bore, but I'm fascinated. This flea market is a microcosm of capitalism. The greed. The acquisitiveness. The bartering."

Sarah raised an eyebrow. "And what would Jung say?"

"I'm serious. This just might be the topic I choose for my doctoral thesis. A psychological profile of a flea market."

"Are you serious?" Sarah asked skeptically.

"Sure. What could be more American?" he responded. "I could do statistical surveys, questionnaires, interviews." He spied Mick among the milling customers and waved to him.

When Mick sauntered over to join them, Jamie bounced over to him and gave him a big hug. "It's Mickey Mouse."

Joey scowled. "He's not a mouse."

"But he's a Mickey."

Charlie asked, "Could I use your flea market for a research study?"

"Sure. If you don't pester the merchants."

"This might work." Charlie took his nephews by the hand. "How about dessert, guys?"

Jamie cheered. Joey nodded solemnly.

"By the way, Sarah, C. G. Jung would have liked it here. The dedicated search for a bargain strips away facades," Charlie said as he walked off.

"No rabbits," she reminded her nephews.

Mick sat on the bench beside her. Though there were people all around, this was the closest they'd come to privacy all day. His thigh brushed hers, and Sarah self-consciously inched away from him on the bench. There was something uncomfortable about being so near to him.

He stared at the drifting bank of clouds. He seemed tired, and Sarah suppressed an urge to reach over and rub the nape of his neck. She noticed that the gray of the skies matched the dark, smoldering color of his eyes.

"We might be having our dinner early," he said. "If it rains, this place will clear out fast."

"Do you ever get tornadoes out here?"

"Sure. They're incredible. If you don't mind getting wet, you can watch the funnels come down from the clouds like fingers."

Sarah shuddered. All too often those dark fingers touched down, felling huge trees and smashing houses into matchsticks. When she first started working at Werner Foundation, she'd been assigned to the department that administered a disaster fund to provide financial aid to home-owners and small businesses. Sarah had seen the effects of tornado devastation firsthand.

"I've been lucky," he said. "Never had tornado damage." He rapped his knuckles on the wooden bench. "Never been hit by lightning."

If she mentioned hail, sleet and snow, the topic of weather would be exhausted. And Sarah was anxious to talk with Mick about other things—his family, and particularly the problems that Lil had mentioned so briefly. Sarah also wanted to discuss Lil, and Jenny's plan to buy and sell.

She heard the low rumble of thunder and looked up to see a brilliant flash of lightning lance the clouds.

"Here it comes," Mick said.

The rain started with a few warning drops. Then a downpour. Mick stepped out from the overhang of the warehouse roof. The sheets of cold rain brought a smile to his lips. In seconds, he was drenched. His T-shirt was plastered against his chest and water streamed through his ponytail. "It's beautiful, Sarah."

"You're crazy!"

In two strides, he was beside her. He grabbed her hand and pulled her away from the shelter. "Come on, Sarah. Get wild with me."

She yanked her hand from him. "No, thank you."

"You're going to get wet, anyway. When you help your sister pack up her things."

Getting wet was one thing; cavorting in the rain was quite another. Still, Sarah stepped forward and held out her hand to catch a raindrop. Quickly she recoiled. "It's cold."

"Not if you move around." He hopped on one foot and then the other in a crazy jig. "It's lovely weather."

"For a duck."

"Come on, Sarah," he teased. "In your heart, you're dying to play in the rain." He held out his hand. "Come out and play."

"You look ridiculous. Go away, Mick. I'm going to wait until this lets up."

He clutched his heart as if stricken, wiping away the raindrops as if they were tears.

"Oh, all right."

She straightened her jacket, turned up the collar and took a huge step forward. The pellets of rain chilled her, and as she began to move back, Mick caught her hand and dragged her away from the shelter of the overhang.

She kicked at a puddle to splash him. And he kicked back. Water slopped over her neat white sneakers. Her socks were drenched. Then, with Mick's encouragement, she stomped around in a high-kicking circle. She hadn't acted this silly in years.

All around them people were rushing, carrying crates and hiding under the cover of umbrellas.

"Throw back your head," he told her. "Hold up your arms and try to touch the clouds."

"You're making a scene."

"Hell, no. The rain is making a scene. And the wind."

She thrust her arms skyward and allowed the large drops to splatter on her upturned face. She tasted fresh rain on her tongue. Rivulets coursed down her arms and over her breasts, and the chill spread delicious tingles through her body. She looked at Mick and laughed. "This is silly. It's crazy."

"It is. Insane."

Lightly he slipped his hand down her arm. "It's beautiful, too. You're beautiful."

"Right." Suddenly bashful, she scuffed the toe of her sneaker in a puddle. "I'd better go and help Jenny."

"When you're done, meet me at the trailer. The key is under the flowerpot."

He spun around, grabbed a heavy box from a passing merchant and vanished into the rain.

Sarah ran toward Jenny's booth, and found her sister struggling with an already sodden cardboard box full of books. Still, Jenny was grinning.

"I made three hundred and twenty-five," she said.

"Great! Now let's get this junk loaded."

Over the pelting rain, she shouted, "If I did this every weekend, every Saturday and Sunday, I could actually save something toward a down payment for a house."

"Wonderful."

Sarah lifted the box of books onto the dolly. Luckily, many of Jenny's other cumbersome treasures had been sold.

"Forget the damn books," Jenny said. "They're only a quarter apiece."

Sarah flicked open the lid. Steinbeck. *The Great Gatsby*. Dickens. These were *her* books. It was criminal to leave them here, drowning the words that had given her such pleasure. Maybe Jenny didn't care, but Sarah would save the books first.

She loaded another box onto the dolly and wheeled it toward Jenny's station wagon, unloaded, then returned to the booth.

The downpour continued through three more trips back and forth. After the third journey, the fun of being out in the rain had become drudgery. Sarah was cold and miserably wet.

After depositing the boys in his van, Charlie joined them and they finished up quickly. Finally Sarah backed away from Jenny's car, waved goodbye and ran toward Mick's trailer.

The key was under the flowerpot, she remembered. But there were twelve earthenware pots lining the front walkway. Sarah hefted one, then another. In her haste, she carelessly broke a pot of red geraniums. She also slipped and fell down hard in the mud beside the walkway before she at last found the key and charged inside.

She slammed the door closed and leaned against it, gasping for breath. It was dark in Mick's trailer but warm compared to the freezing rain outside. The air was scented with a savory fragrance. Homemade spaghetti sauce?

She needed to change out of her wet clothes. Into what? Sarah flicked on the lights. The warm glow from several small lamps flooded the living room of the trailer, which was comfortably furnished. To her left was a small, open kitchen with a huge pot of spaghetti sauce warming on the stove.

Sarah went through the small archway to the bathroom, found a towel and wrapped it around her head, then explored. Mick's bedroom was packed with file cabinets. A computer and an adding machine sat on a desk in the corner. On the bookshelf nonfiction books on accounting and taxes stood side by side with classics and modern fiction. Just like Mick, she decided—a strange mixture of fantasy and business.

Feeling obnoxiously nosy, she slid open his closet doors and looked for something she could change into. Very rude, but she figured it would be far more acceptable than standing around naked. The first thing her hand touched was a long-sleeved velour shirt, and she grabbed it.

As soon as Sarah had changed into Mick's shirt, she heard the front door open.

She popped into the hallway. "Is it okay if I borrow this shirt?"

He pushed a hank of wet hair out of his eyes to gaze at her. "It looks a helluva lot better on you than it ever did on me."

The navy blue velour drooped halfway to her knees and the sleeves flopped over her hands. "I doubt that."

"Oh, yes," he said definitely. "You've got great legs." Before she could make a self-deprecating comment, he added, "Do you want to take a shower?"

"Yes." A shower would feel good. Hot water would be wonderful. Then she remembered that this was supposed to be a business dinner. "No."

He shrugged. "Suit yourself. But I'm getting cleaned up."

When he strode toward her, the trailer felt very small. She had to back toward his bedroom to allow him the space to go past her to the shower. Before she could escape into the living room, Mick was peeling off his shirt in the bathroom.

Mesmerized, she stared at his upper body. His shoulders were well-developed and tanned. The hair on his chest was coal black, thick and full. When he yanked the rubber band from his ponytail and shook his head, his wet hair fell around his neck.

Unaware of her scrutiny, he asked, "Are you hungry, Sarah?"

"Yes, I am." *Hungry for more than food.*

"Why don't you throw on some boiling water for the pasta. The sauce should be ready by now."

He closed the bathroom door, and she stumbled into the small living room. She wanted Mick. Lusted after him.

And her desire was wrong. She shouldn't be here, braless and naked under a velour shirt that displayed her legs. But why not? It wasn't as if she were betraying the Werner Foundation. Mick didn't want the loan. Hadn't he said so? But Mr. Whelan had other plans. And Sarah knew she hadn't done a good job of explaining the loan program to Mick.

Nothing made sense to her anymore. She needed a list. An agenda.

In the kitchen she fumbled through drawers until she found a scrap of paper and a pencil. She scribbled: "1. Explain loan program. 2. Obtain Mick's approval."

What else? Her mind was empty. Hadn't there been a million other things she wanted to talk to him about?

"3. Discuss Jenny's plan. 4. Lil."

She tapped the pencil against the counter. List making had been a good idea. It gave her a feeling of control and order. She could handle this situation. Maybe she could even control her desire.

"Sarah? Did you start boiling the water?"

Turning her head at the sound of his voice, she saw Mick standing in the archway between the bathroom and bedroom—wearing nothing but a towel and a smile.

The pencil between Sarah's fingers snapped. "Water?"

"Yeah. Water for the pasta. I'm starving."

He rubbed his hair dry with a second towel. The first towel, the one that was wrapped around his middle, slipped a notch. And Sarah caught her breath. His body was utterly magnificent—a fact he seemed unaware of as he stood there, nearly naked, casually telling her that the pots and pans were in a cabinet next to the oven.

When Mick strolled toward his bedroom, Sarah gaped at the archway where he'd stood. Had he really just been there with chest bared and muscular arms reaching over his head with a towel? Or was this one of her more vivid fantasies?

She banged around in the cupboard, found a large pot and filled it with water. On the stove top, she turned the flame to high. The blue gas flames were nothing compared to the heat she felt inside.

Business, she reminded herself. *Explain loan program.* That was the reason she was here. *Briefcase.* She needed her briefcase from her car. She went to the door of the trailer and opened it. It was still pouring.

"Sarah?"

She jumped and slammed the door. "Mick."

Thank goodness, he was dressed. In jeans and a full-cut blue cotton shirt with the sleeves rolled up. He was more dressed than she was.

"What are you doing?" he asked.

"I needed something from my car."

"Wait until the rain lets up," he advised. "Are you cold?"

Not a chance. "I'm fine, thank you."

When she noticed that he had her soaking clothing in his hand, she was embarrassed. Like a slob, she'd discarded her clothes on the floor of his bedroom. Her shorts and jacket and top . . . and panties and bra.

Mick carried the dripping mess to the kitchen sink. "I'll rinse these out and we'll throw them in the dryer."

"I'll do it." Sarah darted quickly into the kitchen, almost shoving him aside. She definitely did not want to watch him handling her underthings.

His kitchen was tiny. Sarah couldn't help bumping into Mick as she washed the mud from her shorts and he stirred the spaghetti sauce. The water on the burner had begun to boil, and it seemed as if the steam encircled them in a sultry mysterious mist.

"Excuse me," he said for the tenth time as he reached for the saltshaker.

Mick added salt to the boiling water and threw in the spaghetti stalks. Then he leaned against the counter beside the stove. Sarah was scrubbing her clothing in the sink. He stood for a moment, just watching her. Her arms moved vigorously as she worked at the dirt on her shorts. And her hips wiggled in counterpoint to the motion of her shoulders. Damn, she was sexy. The swaying of her ass beneath the navy velour was the most sensual thing he'd seen in a long time.

Mick folded his arms across his chest to keep from reaching out and cupping her bottom. It was so easy to think of what might happen next—if he fitted her cute little butt against his groin, if his hand slipped around to the front of her body, if he spread her thighs . . .

She whipped around to face him. She wore no makeup, but her ivory cheeks blushed pink. Her brown eyes were huge and luminous. Of course, her hair was a mess, drenched from the rain and not yet combed. But he liked the wildness of it.

"Where's your dryer?" she asked.

Mick pointed. "Around the counter, there's a closet with louvered doors. Washer and dryer are in there."

As she went to deposit her clothes, Sarah decided that she didn't like the way he'd been looking at her. His expression was too much a reflection of the way she'd been looking at him. And this was all wrong. She needed to regain perspective. To get back to her list. *Her list!* She'd left it in the kitchen. If Mick found it, he'd be annoyed.

When she flicked the dryer to On and peeked around the counter again, her fears were confirmed. He held the list in his hand. "What's this?"

"I make lists," she said. Her cards were on the table; there was no point in denying it. "Those are the items I wished to discuss with you tonight."

"Loans?" His annoyance was evident. "When do you quit working, Sarah? In your sleep?"

"It's the way I am."

"And do you always cross every item off your list?"

"No," she said, thinking of his name that had appeared on list after list, day after day. "Some things can't be taken care of in one day."

"Well, then, let's just scratch number one and number two," he said. "I'm too tired to argue with you about loans, and you're sure as hell not going to get my approval on one." He squinted at the third item. "You want to discuss something about your sister, Jenny?"

"She wants to go into the buying and selling of used goods, and she thinks she can make a small fortune doing it. I'm not sure that she comprehends the necessary profit margins per item or per load that would—"

"Hold it, Sarah. This is your sister's idea. Right?"

"Right."

"If you want me to give Jenny some advice, I'll be happy to. But it's a waste for me to tell you, then have you tell her."

"Well, yes. That does seem inefficient."

"So glad you agree." He dashed the pencil lead through number three on her list and moved on to the fourth item. "Lil? What's this about Lil?"

"She concerns me." Sarah came around to the edge of the counter and stood on the carpet just beyond the kitchen linoleum. "Mick, what do you know about her family?"

"Not much. Her parents are divorced."

"What about her friends?"

"One time she stopped by the store with another girl and they giggled a lot. But usually she's alone. God, you're nosy, Sarah." He took a red-and-white checkered tablecloth from a drawer and shook it out with a flourish. "Lil isn't homeless, if that's what you're thinking. I've never seen her on the street. She goes to high school. She's healthy. She dresses weird, but her clothes are always clean."

"Are you aware that she has a gigantic crush on you?"

"What?" He looked genuinely astonished. "Lil? But she's just a kid."

"She's sixteen," Sarah said. "Not a child."

"A crush? I don't think so." His forehead creased in a thoughtful frown as he spread the cloth on the little table. "Sure, Lil hangs around the store a lot. Probably too much. And she's always offering to help. To open the mail. To add up figures in a column for me. I let her use the typewriter in my office for her school papers. But I've never gotten the idea that she thinks of me as anything more than a friend."

"I don't think she's even acknowledged it to herself."

"Maybe this supposed crush doesn't exist."

"Maybe not." She shrugged. "I guess I just wanted you to be aware that Lil might look upon you as more than a friend. So you wouldn't accidentally hurt her."

"Got it," he said, scowling.

Mick was right to call her nosy. Why couldn't she leave well enough alone? Why did she feel obliged to take in every stray? Mick's friendship with Lil was none of her business. Still, she felt compelled to add, "When I was talking to Lil today, I got the idea that she felt very possessive about you."

"When was that?"

"At the playground. When you . . . when you kissed me."

"This morning? That wasn't a kiss."

"It was," she protested. "Your lips didn't just accidentally bump into my face."

He came toward her. With one finger, he tilted her chin up.

When Sarah looked into his eyes, she felt a spark of awareness. It was as if the sensual embers she'd carefully controlled had been ignited into full flame. By Mick.

Mesmerized, she stood as still as a statue.

Then his mouth lightly tasted hers. A delicate touch. A nibble.

Her heart pounded. And when his hand slid down her throat, grazed the tip of her breast, Sarah moaned. Oh, my God, what was happening to her self-control? She shouldn't be doing this, shouldn't be near him, shouldn't be kissing him back.

But she couldn't stop herself. When Mick's arms encircled her, Sarah joined her body with his. She spread her thighs to encircle his leg and tangled her fingers in his damp hair. The thick strands slithered through her hands, creating a tactile excitement she'd never known before.

His tongue parted her lips and entered her mouth. Her breasts were crushed against his muscular chest. He was so hard, and she was filled with desire for his strength.

Then he gently disengaged himself. Though he didn't smile, the look in his eyes showed her that he had savored their intimacy as much as she had.

"That," he said hoarsely, "was a kiss."

6

THERE WAS NO DISPUTING that! Stunned by the effect of the kiss, Sarah stood still, staring at the entrance to Mick's bedroom. Suddenly she wanted him with an intensity she'd never felt before.

But Mick had returned to the kitchen where he was draining the water from the pasta. "It's done," he said.

Did he really expect her to eat now?

"Sit down," he said.

Silently, Sarah took her place at the table. "Mick, I'm—"

"Quiet," he commanded.

He crossed the room and flicked on a stereo.

"Opera?" Sarah questioned.

"Didn't I tell you to be quiet. First, we eat."

"And then?"

He left her question unanswered.

In the center of their table, he'd set a crystal vase, holding a single red rose. He uncorked a Bordeaux wine and poured it into fluted glasses. Then he ladled out plates of pasta and a sauce so thick it oozed.

Mick stood back and admired his handiwork. "No candlelight. I like to see what I'm eating."

"It's beautiful."

"My mother was a good teacher." Mick slid into his chair. "She wouldn't let us eat and run. We had to dine. Or go hungry."

How could he kiss her like that, as if there was no tomorrow, and then dish out spaghetti?

"I always make too much sauce," he said. "I forget that there aren't fifty people sitting down to dinner."

Fine, she thought. If he wanted to play it cool, she'd play along. With a conscious effort, she sat up straight, brought her ragged breathing under control and shoved her fork into the spaghetti. She could make small talk with the best of them.

"Very good," she said. Then she really tasted the flavor of the sauce. "Very, very good. Delicious."

"Thanks. Mama's recipe."

"Do you come from a large family?"

"I'm the oldest of two brothers and three sisters."

"Only six," she tallied.

"Ah, but my father had seven sisters and brothers. My mother was the youngest of ten. All those brothers and sisters have families. Most of them live near Chicago."

"Do you have any family in Denver?"

"Not anymore."

Sarah realized that if she continued to politely question Mick, she might uncover some useful information about his family and discover why he was so reluctant to apply for a loan. Ironically, this evening might turn into a business discussion, after all. "Lil told me a story about your father being in the home construction business. Until about ten years ago. What happened?"

"He was doing real well until then. But he hooked up with a snake who made a lot of promises he never kept. My father lost everything."

"How?" Sarah recalled that era of prosperity. She'd been studying business at the University of Denver and the housing boom had been phenomenal.

"Ten years ago, Denver was in a growth phase. Build-ers couldn't put up houses fast enough. The boom had just begun to sputter," he explained. "My dad was a small contract builder. Custom homes, mostly. Then, this builder/financier put the idea into his head that good old Papa Pennotti could make a fortune if he carried the en-tire cost of luxury condominiums in the foothills. Dad put up everything he owned for collateral."

Sarah winced. Her assertion that Mick needn't worry about using his land as collateral must have sounded cruel and naive.

"It looked good on paper," Mick continued. "Espe-cially when this financier promised to cover the initial cost of development. Even after this guy backed out, it looked like Dad could pull it off. Then the bills came due. And the condos weren't finished."

He spoke in a monotone, as if he'd recited this story a hundred times. "By then, the whole family was in-volved. All my brothers and sisters, even the aunts and uncles back east. They borrowed from banks and foun-dations. They drew from savings. Everybody dribbled in a thousand dollars here and five thousand dollars there. But it wasn't enough. It was a bad investment, bad timing, building problems. Bad luck."

Mick was silent for a while, then went on: "My dad was no Silverado. He paid everybody back, including a huge sum that was interest from the banks. But he lost everything, except for this sixty acres out here in the middle of nowhere that nobody else would buy."

"Did he ever complete the development?"

"Oh, yeah. It's called Winterside."

"But that's a beautiful place," Sarah said. "I've been there. The landscaping is wonderful, and there's a kind of Mediterranean feel to the architecture."

Mick nodded. "I call it Naples on the Platte."

"I'm sure most of those units are sold. How could it have lost money?"

"The selling price per unit turned out to be half what this financier had led my father to expect. But he had to take it. He couldn't carry the interest and penalties anymore. Dad got beaten because of credit."

Which explained a great deal to Sarah about Mick's adamant refusal to finance himself that way. "And your father isn't in Denver anymore?"

"He's retired and living in Phoenix."

"But you stayed here."

"Yeah." Mick didn't want to talk about it. There was no point in rehashing past history. Sure, it would have been nice to finish college. But what was the point in complaining? From early on, he'd learned business lessons that weren't taught in college. An M.B.A. student might hear about duplicity in business dealings, but Mick had dealt with duplicity and, usually, come out on top.

"Mick, what happened to you when your father went out of business?"

"Why do you want to hear this stuff?"

"I'm interested."

She shrugged and he thought the movement appealing.

"How did you end up with a store like Penny Wise?"

"When everybody else went to Phoenix, I stayed behind to clean up the family affairs. Which involved a lot of selling off of possessions. Since I needed to get the best prices, I educated myself about the secondhand market. It's how I got started with the store. After the store was established, the flea market was a natural next step."

"I think you're holding something back, Mick."

"Like what?"

"You've told me the facts of what happened, but you haven't said what it means." She smiled encouragingly. "After all, Mick, you're the guy who drew conclusions from the fact that I saw roses on a cup. Tell me what's behind the facts. I want to know *more* about you."

"Why don't you give me your opinions?"

"Of you?" She dabbed at her lips with a napkin. "All right. I think you like working in the secondhand market because it's outside the system. You're a renegade." Recalling her first impression of him, Sarah added, "Like a pirate."

"But I don't steal from anybody, and that's my rep—my reputation. This rep means I've got to be on my guard at all times, because there's always somebody out there trying to take advantage of me."

"Which means you can't trust anybody?"

"Guess so." Trust was a grand and noble gesture. Unfortunately, he couldn't afford it.

"But that doesn't make sense."

"Why not?"

"It doesn't fit the reality. You might think you're a loner, but you have friends. Every vendor at the flea market respects you."

He tapped his chest and said jokingly, "That's because Pennotti is wise. Penny Wise."

Mick was a complicated man yet he lived by simple rules: Work hard. Take care of yourself. And never trust anybody.

After they'd washed the dishes and settled down with after-dinner coffee, Mick turned the tables.

"We've been talking about me," he said. "Now it's your turn, Sarah. Back at the flea market, when it started raining and you stepped out and played, something happened to you."

"I got wet."

"But that's not all." He grinned. "There was a little flash in your eyes. A kind of glow. Something wild."

Her responding laugh was sarcastic. "Don't start this again, Mick. I am not intriguing. Nor sensitive. Nor a dreamer. And, more assuredly, I'm not wild."

"You're more exotic than you know."

"Am not."

"But you could be," he said, "if you'd let yourself go."

"Why on earth would I want to do that?"

"It's good for you. Hey, I do it. Everybody needs a break from responsibility now and then. Tell me, Sarah, what's the wildest thing you can think of?"

Her mind raced through the possibilities. "Dyeing my hair pink, standing on top of a mountain at midnight, skiing—I do actually ski."

"What else?"

"A tattoo," she said. "Like the lilies on Lil's shoulder. In my book, having a tattoo is wild. And I've noticed that you haven't let yourself go enough to have a tattoo, have you?"

"Yes, I have."

"But I don't see it." And she'd seen quite a lot of him when he'd been standing in the archway clad only in a towel.

Mick hemmed and hawed.

"Where is this tattoo?" she demanded.

"On my left cheek, okay? I have a butterfly tattoo on my butt."

She laughed. "I'm not even going to ask how that happened."

"No big deal. One night I got a little crazy." He studied her. "Now, where are we going to put your tattoo?"

"Don't be silly, Mick. A tattoo is a good illustration of how being wild can hurt you. There's a momentary thrill, then you're scarred for life."

"Not necessarily." Still talking, he disappeared through the archway toward his bedroom. "I can give you a tattoo that washes off, Sarah."

He returned and popped open a small box containing a set of calligraphy pens. "Indelible ink, but it washes off."

"Eventually," she said, recalling the henna mistake.

"Where do you want your non-scarring tattoo?"

"I don't."

"Live a little, Sarah. Be a wild woman."

Wild? Well, yes, it would certainly be bizarre for an executive administrator to march into the Werner Foundation offices with a tattoo.

Mick took her hand in his. "On your wrist," he suggested. "A tasteful rose."

"No. I'd feel silly looking at it all day and explaining."

"Not a butterfly on your bottom?"

Mesmerized by Mick's nearness, she made her decision. Sarah unfastened the top buttons of his velour shirt to bare an expanse of flesh above her breast. "Here," she said.

"Very nice."

His gaze was hot. Very appreciative. Sarah leaned back in the chair and allowed herself to be admired. It had been a long time.

When the tip of his pen touched her skin, she shivered and he warned, "You can't move around, Sarah."

"Right."

But her breath quickened. When his hand accidentally brushed her breast, Sarah gripped the arms of the chair, forcing herself to remain still. Her nipples tightened.

He was so very close. His thick hair smelled wonderfully clean and fresh. The pen tip lightly scratched again, and she had to fight for control.

"Tickles," she said.

"Be still, Sarah."

How could she sit here quietly while his breath warmed, then cooled her? She was all goose bumps. How could she ignore the fact that a very sexy male was touching her breast? Sarah tried to think of other things. But each time the pen pressed down on her flesh, she grew more aroused.

Sarah longed to do something really wild—to sleep with Mick.

She gasped. "Are you done?"

"Not quite."

The tension was unbearable. She closed her eyes and wished she had never suggested a tattoo.

When he blew lightly on her breast, Sarah nearly moaned. Then she felt him moving away. Her eyes opened and she stared up at him. His gaze moved downward to her breast and she looked at his handiwork.

"A unicorn." The tiny blue unicorn shivered as she exhaled the breath she'd been holding. "Thank you, Mick."

He leaned toward her again. His fingers touched her lips. "Stay here with me tonight, Sarah."

"I can't."

She couldn't stay with him. No matter how much she wanted to be wild, Sarah couldn't forget who she was. "It's not the right time."

"Why not?"

She swallowed hard. "You're not going to like what I have to say."

"Is this about items one and two on your list? The loan?"

She nodded.

"Dammit, Sarah." He stood and glared at her. "When are we going to get this thing out of the way? I don't want a loan. I never filled out an application."

"But you did. I have it in my car. In the briefcase."

He stuck out his hand. "Give me your car keys."

"They were in the pocket of my shorts."

He stormed into his bedroom and returned, dangling her keys from their chain. "Where's your briefcase?"

"In the back seat."

He charged out the door. Sarah knew she was doing the right thing. The only ethical thing. Before anything could happen between them, the Werner Foundation business had to be settled.

She moved to the table, which had been cleared, crossed her legs, and waited.

Mick returned with her case and placed it on the table in front of her. "Show me this application."

She opened the catch and found the manila folder with Mick's name printed on the tab. "Here it is." She pulled out the two-page loan application. "A summary of your warehouse project, including approximate costs. Profit-and-loss figures from Penny Wise. Checking-account balances. And the balance—a ridiculously high cash balance—from a savings account."

"No mention of the flea market?"

Sarah frowned. "No. But there is a mention under 'Assets' of sixty-three acres with the designated information from a deed."

"Give it to me."

Sarah handed over the paper. She pointed to the last page, on the dotted line, where Mick's signature had been scrawled.

"I didn't write this," he said.

"Oh, please." How could she believe that? "I can understand if you changed your mind, but don't try to tell me that you didn't fill this out."

"Sarah, this is not my signature. It's not a bad forgery, but I didn't sign this."

His words sank in, but she still refused to accept them. "Who else would have access to this information?"

"It wouldn't be too hard to get. Not if you were familiar with bank practices and loan procedures."

Sarah knew he was right. The data contained in this application was a matter of record. Not easily or ethically available information, but accessible nonetheless. She shook her head. This didn't make sense. "But why would anyone bother to apply for a loan that was meant for you?"

"Maybe somebody who wants to get their hands on my land." Mick laid the document on the tabletop. "I'd have to use this land for collateral. Maybe somebody is setting me up. To seize my property."

As he spoke, a chill went through her. Sarah thought of Mr. Whelan and his unusual interest in Mick's loan. Whelan had said he was familiar with Mick's property. Whelan was involved in the construction industry. He might want this property. But why? The timing wasn't right for a new housing development.

Softly Mick said, "I'm right, aren't I? You know somebody who wants this land."

"No. It's unthinkable." Mr. Whelan was a respected member of the business community. A philanthropist.

"You're lying. I can see it in your eyes."

"I'm not."

She reached for the document, but he pulled it away. "I'll hang on to this, Sarah. Seems to me that forgery is illegal. Hell, this might even be fraud or entrapment."

"That's absurd. I've never handled a loan where collateral was seized. Never. And I've been working in loans for four years."

"Anything of this size?"

"No," she admitted. The largest loan package that Sarah had prepared was fifty thousand dollars. "I'm in small loans."

"Maybe you've just graduated." He folded the document and placed it in his shirt pocket. "Maybe you're going to learn what business is really about. Because it's not M.B.A. stuff, Sarah. Business is dirty. People get hurt."

His words stung. Though she knew he was right, she believed, truly believed, that the Werner Foundation wasn't like other businesses. At the Werner Foundation, they tried to provide financial assistance to people who needed it. Their funds came from people with good motives. Like Mr. Whelan? What did she actually know about him? Other than the fact that he was a member of the board?

"No." She shook her head. "I don't believe it."

"You don't believe me? Well, congratulations, Sarah. You've learned the first lesson in business reality. Don't trust anybody."

DURING HER LONG DRIVE home, Sarah's brain churned with questions. And regrets. She had wanted to stay with Mick. Every instinct urged her stay. But without trust?

His accusation of forgery was absurd. He must have been lying about the signature. But why? And what if he was telling the truth? The prospect horrified her. If Mick had not submitted that document, if Mr. Whelan had been engineering a scheme to take Mick's land, the whole basis of the Werner Foundation was fraudulent. Which meant her career was a joke.

All day Sunday, while Sarah was doing her weekend chores, she wondered and worried. About Mr. Whelan. About the foundation she worked for. And about Mick. Actually, it was impossible to avoid thoughts of Mick because Jenny had undertaken a campaign to convince Sarah to "get serious" about him.

Sunday night, after the kids were in bed, Jenny started in again. "He likes you, Sarah."

"And I like him." Sarah dumped cleanser in the sink and scrubbed. "But there are other things involved."

"Like what? Business? If that's the only thing—"

"Leave it alone, Jenny."

"Just a fling with him," she urged. "What could it hurt?"

Sarah said nothing. The last time she'd accepted her sister's advice, her hair had suffered. This time, it might be her heart.

The next day at work, Sarah attempted to reach Mr. Whelan, to confront him about the forgery. But his secretary at Whelan Resources said he was gone for the day. Sarah frowned. Since most of the board members ran other businesses, it was always difficult to contact them. Only the chairman of the board and the former chairman, Frank Chapperal, kept permanent offices in this building.

Trying to settle down and work, Sarah found herself jumping every time the telephone rang, hoping the caller would be Mick. But his phone call never came. At the end of the day, she wrote a nice, neat thank-you-for-dinner note and dropped it into the mail.

Arriving at home that day, Sarah tried to keep the pitiful note of hopefulness from her voice. "Any calls for me?"

"No," Jenny said. "Didn't Mick call you at work?"

"I don't want to talk about it."

"Oh, Sarah, honey, I'm sorry. I really thought you and Mick were good together."

"Let's just forget it, okay?"

Sarah pried open the refrigerator. Chocolate. She wanted chocolate in chunks. Chocolate had never let her down.

Jenny made an offer. "I just baked some chocolate-chip cookies."

Like the cookies in Mick's store. Sarah almost cried. "No, thank you. I'll just eat this chocolate cake that Charlie had under his armpit the other night." The night that Mick had showed up at the door unannounced.

Sarah went to her room and flopped across the bed. She should forget him, erase him from her mind. And yet, that night before she stepped into the shower, she stuck adhesive strips over the unicorn he'd drawn on her breast, so the colors wouldn't fade.

On Tuesday, Mick still didn't telephone. And Mr. Whelan still wasn't in his office. Sarah worked late.

The moment she entered her house that evening, even before she had a chance to whine about phone messages, Jenny turned her around and pointed her back toward the car. "We're going to an auction."

"I don't want to. I'm tired."

"We're going, Sarah. And bring your checkbook."

"I don't want to buy anything."

"Who said you did? I'm going to do some buying, and I might need a small loan from you." Jenny pushed her toward the door. "Let's go. Charlie has agreed to watch the kids."

Grumpily Sarah slouched down on the passenger side of Jenny's station wagon. An auction? A small loan? She felt as if she was being railroaded. While Jenny chattered happily about the great bargains that had been listed in the newspaper advertisement for the auction, Sarah tuned out.

Of course, Sarah thought, it was great that Jenny had a sense of purpose, but her sister's enthusiasm was annoying. Why did everything work out so well for Jenny? Why did Jenny already have a husband and two kids? All Sarah had was a big, cumbersome house and a job that she didn't know whether she loved or hated.

At a large warehouse building in south Denver, Jenny found a parking place and rushed Sarah inside. "Oh, good," she said. "We're not late. They haven't started."

Jenny found them two seats on folding chairs near the front. Sarah crossed her arms over her chest and eyed the exits longingly. She had no interest whatsoever in being there—not unless someone had decided to auction off a five-pound chunk of chocolate.

Her eyelids closed. Her head nodded forward. She felt Jenny poke her in the ribs and say, "It's starting."

"Oh, great. Wake me when it's over."

The auctioneer's voice boomed over a microphone, "Our first piece is a real winner. From the closeout of Oxmeld Furniture, we have a genuine leather sofa and matching chair. Bidding starts at three hundred dollars."

Sarah snapped awake. She knew that voice. It was Mick's.

Torn between a desire to disappear and a need to jump up and punch him in the jaw, she sat bolt upright.

"Surprise," Jenny whispered.

Mick pointed at Sarah and said, "We have three hundred and seventy-five."

"What?" Sarah turned to Jenny.

"I think you just bid on the sofa."

"But I don't want a leather sofa. I can't afford—"

"Then you'd better not move."

She sat very still while Mick ran through his fast-talking spiel and wound up selling the leather sofa and chair for six hundred and fifty dollars.

He seemed to be looking directly at her when he said the words, "Going . . . going . . . gone."

7

WHILE MICK FAST-TALKED his way through a slick description of another piece of furniture, Sarah hissed at her sister, "Great. Really great. I suppose you think this is cute."

"I do," Jenny complacently replied. "When Mick called me to talk about my—"

"Mick called you?"

"He called to talk about whether or not I wanted to rent a regular booth at the flea market. But he mentioned this auction and hinted that he wouldn't mind seeing you again."

"You should learn to mind your own business."

"It *is* my business," Jenny protested. "When you're miserable, you make all of us miserable."

Mick started his spiel again, and Sarah sat very still, not wishing to risk a bid on a grotesque lamp.

"Sold," he shouted. "To the gentleman in the baby-blue cowboy hat."

In silence, Sarah fumed. If Jenny didn't like her attitude, then Jenny could darn well move out. It was her house, not Jenny's. She was making the mortgage payments plus monthly payments to her parents. And she was fed up with her sister's judgments and interference. When she had offered her hospitality to Jenny and her boys, Sarah had thought the six months would fly past. But this was only month number three, and she felt cramped. She wished everybody would go away and leave her alone—Jenny and Charlie and Charlie's friend, Tim, who didn't seem to be making much effort to find somewhere else to live.

"Going. Going. Gone!" Mick shouted.

When she glared up at Mick, he cocked his finger like a pistol and fired an imaginary bullet at her. His lips mouthed the word, "Later."

Of all the nerve! He couldn't be bothered to telephone, and now he was making a date in the middle of an auction?

Sarah bolted to her feet.

Smoothly, Mick said, "Would the lady in the third row please sit down?"

"No, she won't," Sarah snapped. "The lady is leaving."

Into the microphone he said, "Wait for me, Sarah. I want to see you."

"Hey there, Sarah," teased a stranger from the audience. "Give the guy a break."

"I would," said a woman's voice. "I'd wait forever."

Jenny tugged on her sleeve. "Sit down, Sarah."

She bent her knees and sat.

She avoided looking at the platform where Mick continued with his spiel. A fast talker, all right. Last Saturday night, he had made her think she was special. He'd set a beautiful table. He'd fed her, confided in her. He'd painted a unicorn on her breast. And he'd kissed her.

"Sold," he said.

On Saturday night, she'd almost been sold on him. She'd come close to going to bed with him.

Jenny nudged her elbow and pointed to a note in a flimsy, mimeographed program. "It says here that Mick is only going to be auctioneer for the first two lots of stuff. He ought to be done in a few minutes."

"Then what?" Sarah managed to reply.

"Then he can take you home. You're bored by this auction, and I'm not interested in anything until later, when they're going to sell lots of stuff from the closing of a novelty store."

"I don't want Mick to take me home. And why are you going to buy stuff from a novelty store?"

"To resell, silly."

A tall man behind them tapped Sarah's shoulder and asked if she would please be quiet.

She hushed. Soon there would be a break, and she could flee. But the minutes trickled slowly. The pleated white skirt that she'd worn to work felt rumpled. The waistband was too loose. Her panty hose itched.

Mick certainly put on some performance as an auctioneer. He was marvelously glib. His movements on the platform were quick and agile. With little effort, he lifted a television set over his head to display it. He paced. His arm jabbed forward to point at the bidders. All the while, he easily charmed every person in the audience. Everyone, Sarah thought determinedly, except herself.

"And the microwave oven goes to that distinguished gentleman, Henry Pickens."

White-haired Henry shouted back, "It isn't that I need any help in heating up."

Mick responded, "But I'd heard that you were a slo-o-ow-cooking man, Henry."

"You're right, Mick. I can simmer all day."

His wife chortled. "Like a stew pot."

Mick laughed with her. "That's all for me, folks. Your next auctioneer is Louis Garcia from Alamosa."

There was a smattering of applause. Mick handed over the chrome microphone, hopped down from the platform and came toward Sarah. Amid hoots of encouragement from the audience, he took her hand and led her from the hall. Jenny followed.

Once outside, Jenny got in the first word, "Louis is only doing heavy equipment, right?"

"That's right. Farm implements, mostly."

"Listen, Mick," Jenny said with a perky frown. "I need to go back in. But that means Sarah is stranded here. I'd appreciate if you would give her a ride home."

"I'd be delighted."

Without another word, Jenny strolled back into the auction hall.

Sarah turned to Mick. "I can find my own way home."

"But I'd like to give you a ride."

"No, thank you."

She stalked through the doors to the parking lot behind the auction house. It was dark outside, past nine o'clock. She stared up at the full moon—a lovers' moon.

Mick caught her arm. "We've got to talk."

"Why?" She wheeled around and faced him. "Nothing has changed since Saturday. I still haven't settled this issue of your loan application."

"It's not important."

"You bet it is! For all I know, you might be planning to sue the Werner Foundation. We might be sitting on opposite sides of a litigator's table."

"I don't believe in lawyers."

"That figures." Her frustration soared. "You don't believe in lawyers. Or accountants. Or banks. Or loans. You think you're some kind of noble Lone Ranger, galloping outside the system. Heroic and free. You don't need anybody, right? Well, you don't need me, either."

"That's right. I don't *need* you. But I care about you, and I want to spend time with you."

"Why?"

"Darned if I know." He paused, almost wincing. "That's not true. I want to be with you because I like you. You're easy to talk to. Every once in a while, I see something in you that makes me feel . . . different."

He couldn't explain his feelings about her with the same ease with which he could describe a table or a lamp that was up for bid. He couldn't say why she was so appealing to him. "You turn me on, Sarah."

She scoffed. "Should I say 'Thank you'?"

"I don't care what you say. Just say it to me."

He watched her expression change from anger to confusion. Two parallel frown-lines appeared between her eyebrows, and he wanted to touch them, to stroke her forehead.

"I'll say one thing to you." Her mouth was a tight line. "You drive me crazy, Mick Pennotti. If I excite you so much, why didn't you call?"

"I was too damn mad. That whole business with the loan application pissed me off. It seemed like I was being set up, conned."

"And now?" she questioned. "Now, you're not angry?"

"I don't blame you. I'm sure you didn't know about the forgery."

"How very reassuring." Her tone was sarcastic. She was unappeased. "So you don't think I'm a crook, just stupid. An M.B.A. with no business smarts."

"Hell, no. Why should you question my signature? And even if you did, I've had a chance to study the numbers on that document, and they're pretty accurate."

"All the numbers?"

"That's right. Even the projections on the warehouse."

Sarah was desperate to solve this. In fact, her whole career depended on finding the solution. "I don't get it. There might be a way of finding out your accounting figures for Penny Wise, but nobody could know approximate figures based on your future plans. I assume you don't have those numbers on file anywhere."

"Only in my office at Penny Wise," he said. "The way I figure, somebody went through my office and pulled the numbers they needed for the loan application. That's why there was nothing in that document about the flea market. I keep those records at my trailer."

"Are you suggesting that someone broke into your office and copied down the numbers?"

He nodded.

"But that can't be."

Though Sarah had come to grips with the possibility that Mr. Whelan might have dummied the loan form, she couldn't believe that he'd been a party to breaking and entering. And what did that make Sarah? An accessory to the crime? She swallowed hard. "What are you going to do about it, Mick? Press charges?"

"I don't know."

"You have cause," she said with heavy resignation. "Especially if you think someone broke into your office."

"I'd rather forget the whole damn thing. It's water under the bridge."

She eyed him carefully, trying to read his mood. His expression was as inscrutable as ever, but there was something else in his eyes. A challenge? Her physical response to him was as powerful as ever, and she had to look away. "I shouldn't be talking to you."

"Why not?"

"Because you could sue the Werner Foundation. And I'm right smack in the middle of this. I accepted your package. I presented it to the board of directors. I did follow-up research. All on the basis of a forged signature."

"I'm going to drop this, Sarah. Okay? It's over."

"How can it be over? You still have the loan application."

"If it worries you so much, I'll give the loan application back to you. You can burn the damn thing."

A surge of relief washed over her, and she sighed. She hadn't realized until that moment how important it was for her to have the loan papers back in her possession. "You'd do that? You'll give up evidence? For me?"

He nodded. "Let's go. Right now. We'll go to Penny Wise and get the damn thing."

The fact that Mick was willing to give the application back to her signaled a change between them. They weren't standing on opposite sides anymore. She smiled broadly. "You trust me."

"Yeah, I guess so." His hand swung down and caught hers. "Let's go, Sarah."

"Thank you, Mick."

"It's no big deal."

But it was. She knew that Mick trusted her, and he didn't give his trust lightly. It was a very big deal.

She tagged along beside him to the rear of the parking lot where he halted beside a huge black motorcycle with gold trim. "Where's your car?" Sarah asked.

"No car." He went to the rear of the motorcycle and unlocked a storage compartment.

"A motorcycle?" Sarah gasped.

"A Harley," he corrected.

"But I've never ridden on a motorcycle."

"Nothing to it. You sit on the back and hold on to me."

"I'm not dressed for this."

From the storage compartment, he pulled out a worn leather jacket and tossed it to her. "I need to get another helmet. You stay here, Sarah. I'll be right back."

He jogged toward the auction house, leaving her there.

Timidly she reached out and touched the machine. It was cold and hard.

But as nervous as she was about riding on the motorcycle, she had to do it. Mick had given her his trust and she owed him the same consideration.

Mick returned with a blue helmet, which he pulled over his thick hair.

Then he straddled the Harley and started the powerful engine. "Climb on, Sarah. You're not scared, are you?"

"Of course not." Scared? No, she was terrified. People died on motorcycles; she knew the statistics. And she didn't like speed. And she got motion sickness. A carousel ride was enough to make her vomit.

In a loud voice, Mick explained to her where she should put her feet and where her legs must not touch. Then he took a heavy black helmet from the rear and handed it to her. When she put it on, she found its face-covering shield obscured her vision—definitely a blessing in disguise.

"Climb on, Sarah."

Stiffly she mounted, thankful that her skirt was wide enough that she wouldn't rip a seam. When the Harley vibrated and rumbled beneath her, Sarah shuddered.

"You've got to hold on to me," he shouted. "And don't fight the turns, Sarah. Just lean the way your body wants to lean."

She slid her ducky purse up her arm and placed her hands at his waist. When the Harley bucked into motion, Sarah's arms tightened around Mick. She held on for dear life, trying to bury her face against his back, but the helmet got in the way. She was going to die, she just knew it.

In traffic, her terror magnified. The cars were too close. What was she doing here, anyway? Sarah Mac-Neal was an executive administrator—not a motorcycle mama.

When they pulled up at a stoplight, she peeled her arms off Mick and started to dismount.

"What are you doing?" he yelled.

"I'm getting off this thing."

"You don't like the traffic, huh?" he guessed. "Okay, hold on. We'll take side roads."

When the Harley lurched forward, she resumed her death grip around his torso. Side roads? Why would that be any safer? She could die on a suburban street corner just as easily as she could be killed by the streaming rows of traffic.

But Mick was right. The side roads were quieter, and she relaxed—marginally—as they sped along.

Nevertheless she fastened herself to Mick, determined not to open her eyes or her mouth until she got off this thing. The noise of the Harley engine formed a shell around her, blanking out everything else.

Though Sarah had heard that riding motorcycles could be an intensely sexual experience, she didn't feel aroused. Her legs were jiggling too fast; her arms were sore from hanging on. Even her tight embrace of Mick didn't seem sexy—which was probably because she wasn't thinking of him as a man but as the only thing that stood between life and road kill.

The instant they stopped, she climbed off the Harley, braced herself on weakened knees, yanked off the helmet and looked around. They were in the alley behind Penny Wise.

"Oh, my," she sputtered. "My, oh, my, that was awful."

"Hush, Sarah."

The moment he parked his motorcycle at the rear entrance of his store, Mick knew something was wrong. The alley was too dark. The security light was gone. Broken glass crunched underfoot.

"Damn," he muttered.

The back door to Penny Wise stood wide open.

"There's been a break-in," he whispered. "Go to the gas station on the corner and call 911."

He wheeled his Harley to safety behind a trash bin. "Go, Sarah."

"Not if you're staying here." She ducked down beside him, keeping her eye on the rear of the store. "This could be dangerous."

He stared at Sarah in frank disbelief. What did she plan to do? Beat somebody to death with her ducky purse? "Make the call, Sarah."

"I'm staying with you." She pushed her hair into a semblance of order. "You shouldn't be here by yourself. Either we both go to the corner, or neither of us goes."

Her mind was made up, and that was that. Mick sighed. "You sure picked a helluva time to be tough."

"I don't want you to get into a fight where you might be outnumbered or the other people might be armed, or they might—"

"Then hold it down. If anybody's in there, you're going to scare them off."

"As if they didn't notice the sound of the Harley?"

"You're right." He stopped whispering. "Nobody's inside."

But when he reached for the Harley's handgrip, she clasped his arm and pulled him back into the shadows. "Look."

A small figure emerged from the store. A quavery voice called out, "Mick? Mick, are you out here?"

When he stepped out from behind the trash bin, the figure jumped and gave a little screech.

"It's okay, Lil. Only me. Mick."

With red hair flying, Lil ran to his arms. As he held her against him, Mick felt her trembling. "It's okay," he soothed. "Just relax."

"I saw them," she said. "Those two guys who got arrested in your store. The tall scary one. And his musclebound friend."

"Did you call the police?" Sarah asked.

"No." Her eyes were wild and frightened as she looked from Mick to Sarah and back again. Lil hiccupped a sob and snuggled closer to Mick. "No police."

Though Sarah didn't want to believe that Lil had anything to do with the break-in, she was suspicious. It was almost ten o'clock at night. And Sarah had seen Lil come from the rear entrance. If Lil was innocent, why didn't she want to call the police?

"I'll go now and call," Sarah said.

"No. Please, no," Lil wailed. "I snuck out of the house. If my dad finds out, he'll kill me."

"Calm down." Mick stroked her back. "Why did you sneak out?"

"I do that sometimes. Okay? I go out and walk around. Sometimes, I get a can of pop and sit at the bus stop across the street and drink it. That's what I was doing. Just hanging out and kind of looking at the store.

Then I saw somebody inside." She looked up at him. "I thought it was you, Mick. So, I came across the street and peeked in the window. And I saw those guys."

"You shouldn't have gone inside," he said. "You could have been hurt."

"I didn't go in right away. I came around back and waited until they left. Then I didn't know what to do. I figured I'd go in and see if they did anything really terrible. Maybe I kind of thought I'd clean up."

"I'm going to call the police now," Sarah insisted. "This is a burglary, and we need to file a report. I'm sure Mick's insurance company will require police verification."

"I've got to go," Lil said.

Mick knew she wasn't faking panic. But it wasn't going to help his situation if she took off. "You need to talk to the police, Lil. You're a witness."

"I won't do it. My dad would be so mad."

"You'd be doing the right thing," Sarah encouraged. "You'd be helping Mick."

She broke away from Mick. "You can't make me do it."

"You're right, I can't force you to come forward. But dammit, Lil, these guys need to be put away. Everybody knows they're behind the robberies along Colfax. But they're pros. They don't leave prints. No evidence. You're the first person who has actually seen—"

"I'm sorry, Mick." She whipped around and sped down the dark alley. In an instant, she was gone.

"Now?" Sarah asked. "Should I go to the corner and call?"

"Since there's nobody inside, we might as well use the phone in the store."

Sarah fell into step behind him. Had Lil really been involved in this break-in? She could easily believe the story about Lil sitting across the street and staring at the store.

After all, the girl had a crush on Mick, and Sarah recalled doing similar silliness in her own teen years—walking past her boyfriend's house and sighing.

But Sarah couldn't believe that Lil went into the store to clean up. And even if she was afraid of the police, she could have placed an anonymous call.

When Mick flicked on the lights, the damage wasn't readily apparent. The store had not been ransacked.

"Pretty tidy thieves," she remarked. "Can you tell what's missing?"

"I can guess." He went to the cash register. The drawer had been sprung open. All the money was gone.

Without a word, Mick strode to a door with the word Office stenciled on it in old-fashioned script. The lock had been broken.

He pushed open the door and turned on the light.

"Very professional," he said. "They didn't bother blowing the locks. They carried off the whole damn safe."

"Oh, Mick. I'm so sorry. What was in there?"

"Over five thousand in cash." His fist crashed down hard on the desktop. "Damn."

"Why so much? Good Lord, Mick, why don't you keep your money in a bank?"

"This is a cash business, Sarah. Most of the time, I make my buys in cash."

"But five thousand dollars?"

"It's not usually that much," he admitted. "I was going to make a good-sized buy tomorrow. On an estate. There are a couple of people in the bidding, and cash talks louder than a check." He sank into the chair behind his old wooden desk. "Let's not mention Lil to the police, okay?"

She reluctantly agreed. "Okay, it's your decision. But Lil told us that she saw the thieves. She could make an identification."

Sarah punched out 911 on the office telephone. At least the robbery wasn't Lil's doing; there was no way that skinny Lil could carry off a safe.

"Before the patrol car gets here," Mick said, "I ought to explain something, Sarah. I'm not exactly a favorite of the Denver Police Department. They seem to think that all secondhand stores are fronts for fencing operations."

"Why?"

"Makes sense, doesn't it? I buy used merchandise. Which could be stolen. Of course, I check identification. And I file all the resale forms. And I don't take used television sets or other obvious theft items. But there's always the possibility that somebody has passed me a set of silverware that wasn't handed down from their grandmother in the Old Country."

"It sounds like you're doing everything right," she said. "Why would the police dislike you?"

"I have a low tolerance for being hassled."

After Sarah told the 911 operator about the robbery and gave the address of Penny Wise, she turned back to Mick. "You do have insurance, don't you?"

"Sure." His eyes were distant and cold. "Not that it's going to do me a damn bit of good. You're the expert, Sarah. Is an insurance company going to take my word for how much cash was in the safe?"

"But I'm a witness to the fact that there was a break-in. Surely you have bank records that verify a cash withdrawal." Sarah knew he was right. Insurance policies generally stipulated a limit on replacing a cash loss in a case of robbery. And that limit fell far short of five thousand dollars.

The whine of a police siren prevented further conversation. The flashing of red and blue whirling lights glared through the rear door of the shop.

A burly cop with a hand on the butt of his pistol was the first to enter. He lumbered through to the center of the store and looked around. "So? Looks the same as usual in here. How can you tell when something's missing from this rathole?"

"I keep records," Mick replied. "Real good records."

"Yeah? Doesn't your hair get in your eyes?"

His partner had followed him into the store, and they shared a smirk over that dull joke. "Okay, Pennotti," the first cop said. "What's gone?"

"Money from the cash register. The safe from my office." He paused before adding, "And a keyboard synthesizer."

8

THOUGH THE POLICE dusted for fingerprints and filed reports on the robbery, Sarah recognized the futility of those exercises. Mick's money was gone. And without Lil's testimony, there was little chance that he'd ever see one penny—wise or unwise—again.

After the police left, Mick sprawled back in his chair with his feet propped on his desktop. He sighed and stared up at the acoustic-tile ceiling. Sarah perched opposite him, wishing there was something she could do to help.

"I'm sorry," she whispered.

"Why? This isn't your fault."

"You know what I mean. I'm sorry this happened to you."

"Yeah, I know." He counted the dots in the ceiling tile. "Bad luck. Bad timing. I usually wouldn't have more than five hundred bucks in the safe."

The policemen hadn't believed him when Mick told them he had five thousand dollars in his safe. They'd noted the information and exchanged a smirk. Sarah had gotten the distinct impression that the two patrolmen thought Mick had faked the robbery.

"We should have told them about Lil," Sarah said. "She's a witness. She could identify the thieves."

"I know who robbed me. It was the two guys who were in here before," he said. "The two that Eddie and his partner picked up on that first day you came here."

"The police already said they'd check them out. Maybe they'll—"

He lifted his feet off the desk and his shoes hit the floor with a crash. He leaned forward. His eyes were hard. "Give it up, Sarah. This isn't a cop show on TV, and those cruds aren't going to be caught. They didn't leave fingerprints. There's no evidence."

"There's Lil," she persisted. "An eyewitness."

"Well, she's not exactly reliable. Can you see her on a witness stand? A sixteen-year-old who hangs out at a secondhand store and has a tattoo. It'd take a lawyer two minutes to get Lil to admit that she'd do anything for me—including lying."

Sarah refused to believe there was nothing that could be done. "What about the missing electronic keyboard, Mick? Do you think Lil was involved in the robbery?"

"I think she took the keyboard," he admitted.

"Lil sometimes helps with your accounting. Would she have known about the money in the safe?"

"I took the money out of the bank today. Nobody knew about it. Nobody but me."

Sarah was grasping at straws. "All right. Then we should review your bank records. At least the records will show your cash withdrawal."

"But they won't prove that I didn't steal it from myself," he said angrily. "*Your* system, Sarah, doesn't work. It isn't fair. The men who robbed me won't be caught. Even if they are, I'll never see my cash again."

"But the insurance—"

"Oh, I'll file a claim. And we'll fight over it. And they'll probably pay me something. But I won't get it all back. And if Lil was mixed up in this—" his brow creased in a frown "—there's not a hell of a lot I can do about it."

"If Lil had something to do with this robbery, she'll tell you. She cares about you, Mick."

"Sure, but the kid isn't exactly a Sunday-school graduate."

"She'll bring the keyboard back."

"How can you be so sure?"

"I'm not. But I think she will. I believe she only borrowed it."

Mick shoved his chair away from the desk. He needed to move, to run. To punch something. And he sure as hell didn't need Sarah, sitting there with her hopeful little plans.

"When are you going to understand?" he demanded. "The system doesn't work for people like me. The only way I'll get my cash back is to find those guys myself and beat it out of them."

"The system can work, Mick. We can make it work."

"How? This store gets robbed once a year. And the cops have never caught anybody who did it."

"You've got to trust *something*."

"Why bother? People lie to me every day. They come in here with phony original Picassos and stainless steel that they claim is silver. People lie. They steal. They cheat."

"I'm not naive," Sarah said quietly. "I know these things happen."

"But not to you. Right? Not in your tidy life."

"That's enough, Mick." She stood and glared at him. "Your life is different from mine, but you're not the only person in the world who has been cheated and betrayed. You were so concerned about the forged signature that you didn't even notice that I'm affected, too. Your loan application came to *my* desk. I presented it. I was duped into believing in your project. And, in case you haven't noticed, it's my job that's on the line."

He yanked open the second drawer of his desk, fished under some papers and pulled out the forged loan application. He handed the document to her. "This lets you off the hook."

She picked up the papers, folded them and filed them in her purse before looking back at him. "I'm sorry about everything." Reaching for the telephone, she said, "I'll call a cab."

"Wait." He couldn't let her walk out of his life. Maybe there was hope, after all.

His hand caught hers and she looked into his eyes. "Yes, Mick? What is it?"

He took a deep breath and glanced at the empty spot on the hardwood floor where his safe had once stood. "I'll handle this. I'll survive. But right now, I'm too damn mad to think about it. I want to break something. To yell. To run for fifty miles without stopping."

"Perhaps a ride on your motorcycle would help you relax."

"Maybe. Come with me."

Sarah gulped. "Gee, I don't know. It's awfully late."

"Don't you trust me, Sarah?"

Before she could come up with a good excuse, they'd left Penny Wise. Mick fastened the temporary lock on the rear entrance and went to his Harley. "You remember how to do this, don't you?"

"Sure," she muttered. "Hang on tight and pray."

Once again, she swung her leg over the rear of his bike and wrapped her arms around him. Her terror about riding on the back of a motorcycle had faded to plain fear.

On this ride, she was occasionally able to open her eyes, peering through the helmet's shield to watch the lights of Colfax Avenue whiz past in a dizzying blur. Through detours and dips and swoops, she clung to him so tightly that her arms were numb. Then they were on a highway, a ribbon of pavement that furled endlessly into the darkness. The night wind became a frigid, battering force.

She knew they were headed west toward the mountains and she hoped—with every shred of hope she had—that they would stop soon. Her arms weren't strong enough to make it much farther. Finally, Mick swiveled off the road and parked.

Sarah opened her eyes. Looming above them were steep, rugged cliffs. Down a sloping hill, she saw the moonlit glimmer of Clear Creek.

Mick dismounted and lifted her from the rear of the Harley. "This was a good idea. I always feel better in the mountains."

"Me, too."

But her knees trembled. Her entire body shook as if she'd been through the spin cycle of a washing machine.

Mick seemed oblivious to her discomfort. Tilting back his head, he gazed up at the night sky. "It always seems like there are more stars up here. Billions of diamonds in the sky."

"Yes, indeed." Sarah yanked off her helmet and plopped down on a nearby rock, not caring that she'd ruin her panty hose or that her pleated white skirt would be filthy.

He hunkered down beside the rock where she was sitting. Though they were only fifty yards from the road, the sheltering mountains and the rushing sound of the stream created an atmosphere of seclusion. When his hand rested on her knee, Sarah tried to control the trembling in her leg.

"You're shaking," he said.

"Am I?"

"I guess riding on a motorcycle was too wild for you."

"Not at all," she lied. "I'm as crazy and spontaneous as the next executive administrator."

Chuckling, Mick asked, "How's my tattoo, wild woman?"

"Still there." In her showers and baths, Sarah had taken extreme precautions to preserve the tiny unicorn on her breast.

"May I see?"

Though she murmured a protest, she was still too weak from the motorcycle ride to object when he eased the worn leather jacket from her shoulders. The cool mountain air seeped through the fabric of her blouse.

Mick unfastened the top two buttons in order to inspect his handiwork, then lightly nuzzled the soft flesh above it.

Her breath caught in her throat. Though Sarah was tired and hadn't slept well since last Saturday night, his kiss sent a thrill racing through her body. She arched her neck, welcoming Mick's attentions. But when she bent to embrace him, she couldn't; their position was too awkward.

Mick slipped his arm beneath her knees and cradled her shoulders. Rising to his feet he lifted her and held her suspended.

Her arms circled his neck. "What are you doing?"

He turned to the right and then the left. "I'm looking for a place to put you where your clothes won't get ruined."

"Forget the skirt," she told him. "I'm a wild woman, remember?"

He strode over to a cottonwood and carefully lowered himself, with Sarah still in his arms. He then positioned her on his lap and leaned his back against the tree trunk.

"Not real comfortable," he said. "I'd rather be in a king-size bed with satin sheets."

"Me, too." Playfully she kissed his cheek.

"I know this isn't the right place, but I want to make love to you, Sarah."

She looked away, and he wanted to shake her, to force her to look at him. "Sarah, I want you."

"And I want you, too. But I can't make love to you—I shouldn't even be here with you—until our business relationship is completely severed."

"What business relationship? I never asked for a loan."

"That's true. But I met you through the Werner Foundation. Ours is a business association."

He stroked the side of her face. Her skin was satiny, her body, soft and supple. "Pretend that you met me tonight."

"But that's a lie."

"No, it's a dream."

When he kissed her, her lips parted, welcoming him. His hand sought her breast, cupped the soft mound of flesh and its tiny peak. His thumb flicked her nipple to taut arousal.

He drew one knee up then, causing her to lean against him. He was hard and his groin was heavy with need—for her.

And she responded, moving her body sinuously, stretching out against him. Her legs spread and she straddled his upraised thigh. He knew she wanted him.

Suddenly the headlights from a car on the highway shone on them. The flash startled Sarah and she slipped from his lap, landing in a clumsy sprawl on the buffalo grass and hard granite.

"Are you all right?" he asked.

"I'd be fine—" she heaved a deep breath "—if I didn't have this rock embedded in my bottom."

Another car sped past.

"Mick, this isn't the right time or place for us to . . ."

"To make love?"

He rose to his feet and held out his hand to pull her upright. When she was standing, brushing the dirt from her skirt, his gaze lifted to the stars overhead. This wasn't the right time. But the moment was coming. And it was coming soon.

"Are you still angry about the robbery?" she asked.

"More than that. I'm frustrated."

She smiled. "There's a creek at the bottom of this hill if you need a cold shower."

"Very funny, Sarah."

"What about that screaming you wanted to do?" she reminded. "In the store you said you were so angry that you wanted to yell or to punch something."

"I'm not angry anymore."

"I am," she said quietly. "There's always something between us. Either it's not the right time. Or not the right place."

"You're frustrated, too."

"Maybe I am." She threw back her head and yelled, "And I don't want to be!"

The mountain breeze whisked her words away. She laughed. "Your turn, Mick."

He looked up. All those untouchable stars. Unabashedly Mick howled at the full moon like a mournful coyote. When he paused to draw breath, he heard Sarah's harmonizing yodel. His voice joined with hers, echoing in the canyon.

His cry became more guttural. He wished all the complications would be gone. Then there would be no robbery. No secondhand junk. Money would be unimportant—as long as he had his woman at his side. Sarah? His woman?

Their voices faded and they stood together quietly. When he looked at Sarah and saw her shiver, he felt protective. "I'd better take you home," he said. "It's late."

"And I have work tomorrow."

But she made no move.

"Sarah? We need to go."

She looked at him. "Couldn't you carry me? I don't want to ride on the motorcycle."

"But you're getting so much better at it."

"I am? How can you tell?"

"On the last couple of miles up here, your death grip around my chest loosened enough so that I could actually breathe."

With a sigh, she mounted the beast. Sarah felt absolutely spent—so tired that she could barely summon the ergy to blink. On the plus side, her exhaustion meant was more relaxed about the Harley. The ride back was tolerable.

When Mick parked the machine in front of her house, Sarah yanked off her helmet. "Would you like to come in for coffee and something to eat?"

"You're tired. Maybe I should just go."

"I insist. All night, I've been wanting to do something for you. If I can't catch the bad guys and recover your five thousand dollars, at least let me feed you."

"You've got a deal."

As she strolled up the sidewalk to her front porch, Sarah noticed that Jenny's station wagon was in the driveway. When she entered the house, she found Jenny sitting at the dining-room table with papers strewn about.

"Well, well," Jenny teased, "you two must have taken the long way home."

Not in the mood for her sister's perkiness, Sarah stalked through the dining room on her way into the kitchen. "We stopped at Mick's store. He'd been robbed."

"How awful!" Jenny pushed out a dining-room chair with her toe. "Sit down, Mick, and tell me about it."

In the kitchen, Sarah brewed some coffee, then opened the refrigerator and stared inside. It wasn't until she'd come into the house and seen Jenny that she realized what she wanted. She longed to be alone with Mick. In her bed.

But now there was Jenny—bright-eyed and bubbly and very much in the way. Sarah grabbed a package of bagels, a jar of mayo and a head of lettuce from the fridge and went to the cupboard to find a can of tuna. Why couldn't her sister have been sound asleep and out of the way? Was that so much to ask? A little privacy in her own home?

Slapping together three sandwiches, Sarah returned to the dining room as Mick was completing his story.

"And that's it," he said. "I expect occasional downturns. And losing five thousand dollars isn't going to kill me. But it's going to make things tight. I'll have to dip into the money I had set aside for the warehouse project."

Sarah set the plateful of bagel sandwiches in front of him and glared pointedly at her sister. "Would you please excuse us?"

"In just a minute. I have a couple of questions to ask Mick, then I'll leave you alone."

Jenny's "couple of questions" stretched into a dissertation, complete with scribbled charts and graphs showing how much she'd spent at the auction and how much profit she could expect on the sale of those various items.

Silently, Sarah leaned her elbow on the table and propped her head on her fist.

"That's enough," Jenny finally said. "I can see that you're both exhausted. I'll say good-night. Don't stay up too late."

"Good night."

Jenny turned at the stairway and beamed. "You two make a darling couple." Then she scampered up the stairs.

After a long yawn, Sarah allowed her head to droop forward onto the tabletop. "She's a great sister. And I adore my nephews. But they're driving me crazy."

"Tell them to move out." His hand glided up her back and began to massage. "You're not your sister's keeper."

"No, but I can't just throw her out on the street."

"Kind Sarah." He kneaded the muscles in her shoulders. "When do you get something for yourself?"

"Soon." She turned in her chair and met his gaze. "Very, very soon."

"On Friday afternoon," he said, "I'm going to be tagging items for an estate sale." He picked up the pencil Jenny had left behind and scribbled an address on one of Jenny's scraps. "Meet me there. As soon as you get off work."

She smiled at him. "That might be soon enough."

He winked. Almost grinned. "Get some sleep."

She could only nod.

He let himself out, and Sarah listened for the roar of his Harley. How amazing that she'd ridden on the back of a motorcycle!

FRIDAY WAS SLOW in coming. And when finally Friday arrived, Sarah was unable to escape from her office. First there was an endless, tedious staff meeting, then a stream of phone calls.

At five o'clock she gathered a stack of work for the weekend and stuffed it into her briefcase. When she looked up, Donald Whelan stood in her office doorway.

"I'm sorry, Sarah, that I couldn't meet with you earlier this week. My schedule didn't permit it."

"I'm sorry, too." As much as she'd been waiting for this confrontation since Monday, she felt unprepared. The situation was so very volatile. She needed to find out if Whelan was responsible for the forgery. But how? She certainly couldn't ask him outright. "Please sit down, Mr. Whelan."

He sat. In his hand he squeezed the same little rubber ball. "Give me your progress report on Pennotti."

"Mr. Pennotti is opposed to taking a loan. He's unwilling to even discuss the possibility. In my opinion, he has good reason to refuse any association with the Werner Foundation."

"Why is that?"

"The signature on his loan application is a forgery. Mr. Pennotti did not authorize us to look into his project." She studied Whelan's features, hoping for a sign that would signal his involvement in the forgery. His interest in Mick's land made him the most likely suspect. But there wasn't a trace of guilt in his expression. "I showed Mr. Pennotti the application. He denies signing it."

"He's lying. I don't know what his game is, but he filed an application. We saw it. You verified the numbers, didn't you?"

"The numbers are correct. The signature was forged."

"Why?" Whelan seemed genuinely astonished.

"I don't know. Possibly, the person who faked the application has reason to believe Pennotti will be overextended. And that his land, which will be used as collateral, will become available."

"If that's what you think, you're as crazy as this Pennotti guy." Whelan picked an invisible piece of lint from his tailored suit. "It seems to me that you're having a problem with this project, Sarah. I'd better assign someone else."

"You can't do that." Sarah bristled. There were only five other people in her department, and Sarah was much more experienced than any of them. "It's not your responsibility as a member of the board to function in administrative affairs."

"A formality. I'll take my thoughts to the board, and the board will approve them."

He was probably right. And Sarah wasn't sure that she wanted to lay this entire affair with Mick before the board.

"I was thinking of Ray Innis," Whelan said briskly.

Ray had been with Werner Foundation less than a year, but he was thorough, competent and career-oriented—as crisp as the starched white shirts he always wore to work. Sarah couldn't imagine anything more disastrous than Ray's strictly-business attitude coming into contact with Mick.

"Mr. Whelan, that would be a mistake."

His shoulder flexed as he squeezed the rubber ball. "You've failed to get results on this project."

"How about this for a result? Mr. Pennotti does not intend to sue the Werner Foundation. Even though he suspects that the only way someone could have filled out the loan papers was to burglarize his offices."

"That's bull!" Whelan stood. "I've had enough of this. Give me the loan application, Sarah."

"No."

His fist tightened. "What did you say to me?"

"I can't let you do this. The Werner Foundation could be liable for invasion of Mr. Pennotti's privacy. Not to mention breaking and entering. I will not relinquish this file to you—or to Ray Innis or anyone else—until the situation has been explained to the rest of the board."

"You're fired."

"You don't have the authority to fire me, Mr. Whelan."

"I have donated a lot of money to this foundation. I can do whatever I please."

He turned and strode angrily out of her office.

Sarah sank down in her chair and closed her eyes. Whelan's threat was not an idle one.

9

DONALD WHELAN didn't have the official authority to fire her. Still, he was powerful, and—as he'd reminded her—he didn't get to where he was by backing down. If he wanted her fired, she would be fired. She sighed. It might be better to resign than to leave with the stigma of dismissal hanging over her.

Spending the evening with Mick probably wasn't the smartest professional move she could make at this time. But what difference could one more night make?

Sarah parked on the street in front of the address Mick had given her. The narrow two-story house with charcoal trim didn't look as if it could be anything as important as an "estate."

She rang the bell, and Mick appeared in the doorway, grinning from ear to ear.

"Bonanza!" he said. "This place is a treasure!"

"I'm glad somebody's happy," she muttered.

"Aw, Sarah." He joined her on the porch. "What's the matter? Did you have a bad day at work?"

"Yes." She squared her shoulders. "But I don't want to talk about it."

"Fine with me."

He took hold of her hand and led her to a porch swing where they sat, side by side. Casually, Mick draped his arm around her.

"I really don't want to discuss it," she repeated.

He patted her shoulder. "That's okay."

They rocked gently, and Sarah tried to unwind, enjoying their companionable silence.

When she felt totally loose and cosy, she turned to Mick and asked, "Anything from your insurance company?"

"I filed the forms."

"How's Lil doing?"

"I haven't seen her. I wanted to call her, but—it's a crazy thing—I don't even know her real name. I've always called her Lil because of her tattoo."

"I hope she's all right."

"Me, too."

"You know, Mick. I've been thinking about the missing keyboard synthesizer. Since it's one of the few electronic items in the store, it might be possible that the thieves took it. Wouldn't they be able to sell it easily to a fence?"

"Sure. But you and I both know that's not what happened." He shook his head. "Lil took the keyboard."

Talking about Mick's concerns resurrected her own. What would Frank Chapperal say about Whelan's accusations? Frank had been chairman of the board until this year, and he'd worked closely with Sarah on a couple of projects. He was a founding member of the board, still kept an office at the Werner Foundation. More than that, Sarah knew he was an honorable businessman. He'd be appalled by the forgery. If only she could talk to him . . .

"Mick! I need a telephone!"

"Sorry. The phones in this house have been turned off."

She bolted from the swing. "I've got to find a pay phone. I'll be right back."

"Sarah!" When she turned around, he flipped her a quarter for the phone. "Good luck, babe."

She ran to her car and drove to a phone booth outside a neighborhood drugstore. After flipping through the white pages, she found the listing for Chapperal. Frank Chapperal answered the phone. "Hello?"

"I'm sorry to bother you at home, Frank. This is Sarah MacNeal from the Werner Foundation."

"Hello, Sarah. How have you been?"

"Fine, thank you. But I have a problem at work. It has to do with Michael Pennotti."

"The warehouse project," he said.

With a huge sense of relief, she explained the situation, carefully avoiding any hint of suspicion about Whelan. She concluded, "I firmly advise that we drop this project."

"The name of his store is Penny Wise?" Was there a chill in his voice?

"Yes. Are you familiar with it?"

"I just might be." He hesitated. "I'm glad to have this information, Sarah. Sounds to me like you've done a good job of handling a difficult situation."

"Thank you, Frank."

She hung up the phone, marched into the drugstore and bought herself a bag of chocolate kisses—celebration chocolate. Finally she'd figured out the right thing to do. There were fifteen members on the Werner Foundation board, and Whelan was only one of them.

Elated she returned to the "estate" and rang the bell.

Mick opened the door and yanked her inside. "Get your cute little butt in here. Do you want to talk?"

"Yes. No. Not really." She'd done enough explaining for one day. "Everything is terrific."

"Good. And did I mention that this average-looking estate is a treasure?"

"Yes."

"This bid was sheer luck," he continued, and there was no mistaking his enthusiasm. "An attorney I'm friendly with telephoned and told me that the heir wanted to get rid of everything fast. The lawyer advised me to bid high, and in cash. And he was right. This time it paid off."

"What's so fabulous in here?"

"The deceased was a ninety-four-year-old woman who had formerly been an opera singer. There are closets full of vintage clothing, gloves, hats, and costume jewelry. And the stuff has been so beautifully taken care of that it could be worn to tonight's performance of *Madama Butterfly*."

"That does sound enticing."

"The large furnishings are definitely resalable." He gestured toward the living room. "My kind of stuff— good secondhand tables and chairs. And a couple of fine antiques, like two Chippendale side tables in mint condition, which I've already taken to an antique dealer."

Many of the chairs and tables were already tagged with Mick's resale prices.

"I've completed a log of the items," Mick said. "Now, I need to figure prices and to slap stickers or tags on everything. Since I'll be at the flea market tomorrow, I have a helper who'll be running the open-house estate sale."

"What can I do?" she asked.

"I'd like for you to sort through the wardrobe in the upstairs bedroom. There are racks on the landing to hang things on."

Sarah gave him a crisp salute and ascended to the second floor. In the large master bedroom, a window fan ruffled the lace curtains. The room smelled like lavender.

The door of a walk-in closet stood open, and Sarah peered inside. Several large garment bags had been unzipped, revealing tantalizing glimpses of frothy pastels and shimmering taffetas. She took out one of the dresses—a pale blue chiffon with a dropped waist. When Sarah held the dress up to her shoulders, it appeared to be just about her size.

She continued unpacking dresses—discovering a lovely coral-pink silk, a sexy red sequined ballgown and several black daytime dresses. She draped the garments around the bedroom, allowing them to air.

When she changed from her business garb into the shorts and T-shirt she had in her briefcase, Sarah felt like a weed in a garden of satin and silk flowers. Gathering up the dresses one by one, she hung them neatly on the racks in the upstairs landing.

In boxes, she found barely-worn pumps and stiletto-heeled shoes in colors to match every dress.

And there were hats—toques and turbans and wide-brimmed picture hats.

But to Sarah, the gloves were the most fascinating item. She very seldom wore gloves, other than to keep out the cold in winter, and she couldn't resist slipping her fingers into a pair of white, wrist-length gloves in see-through lace.

She ran downstairs to show Mick. He was in the living room, sorting through china plates that had been stored in a sideboard buffet. A stack of yellowed cardboard boxes caught Sarah's eye. "Puzzles!"

"Apparently this lady shared one of your hobbies. She had quite a stockpile of picture puzzles."

"I like this one," Sarah said. The cover illustration was a reproduction of a Degas painting of ballerinas *à pointe*.

"It's yours," Mick told her. Then he noticed her gloves. "I see you're really getting into the merchandise."

She made a dismissive gesture and plopped down on the floor beside him. "Tell me about the lady who owned this stuff. She was an opera singer, and what else?"

"According to my friend, the attorney, she was married once, late in life, to a violinist. And she always lived in this house. No children. Her name was Clara." He looked at her. "Which rhymes with Sarah."

"Clara," she said softly. She wondered what Clara's life had really been like. Why did she wait so long to get married? "Where's her piano? If the lady was an opera singer, why no musical instruments?"

"I asked about that. Because pianos are good resale items. The attorney told me that she quit singing when she was sixty and got rid of everything from her former career."

"She must have been bitter," Sarah said with great certainty. "Clara had devoted her life to her career and wound up an old woman with no children to keep her company."

Her analysis of Clara's life seemed to point to an uncomfortable resemblance to her own situation. Though she had plenty of company from siblings who wouldn't leave home yet, what about later, when they'd all gone? She'd assumed that by now she'd be married and have kids. She'd been engaged twice. But both times the wedding plans had fallen through; and she'd been glad when they did. Those men—the two men she thought she loved—hadn't been right for her. Jenny had said she was being too picky. Like Clara perhaps?

"Maybe Clara gave up her music when she found true love."

"Doubtful. He died after they'd been married only a few years. He left her a lot of money."

Poor Clara. She'd waited and waited, only to be disappointed. But at least she'd had a grand passion.

Such a love affair must have given meaning to Clara's life. It must have. Sarah had to believe that life-shaking passion was worth any risk. Being here with Mick wasn't prudent or wise, but she considered her time with him to be precious. She could always find another job, but there would never be another man like Mick in her life. "Do you ever want to get married?"

"Sure. Someday. Coming from a big family, I'd like to have kids. Someday. And you?"

"I'd like to have kids." She stared down at the ballerina puzzle. "I don't know why I'm talking about this. I never do."

"Maybe the spirit of Clara is hanging around in this house, reminding you not to wait until you're sixty to fall in love."

"Her spirit?" Dusk had settled over the house, and the shadows made Sarah wonder.

Mick gave her a long, scrutinizing look and went back to itemizing Clara's goods. He carefully placed a stack of china plates on the sideboard. "I'm almost finished here. How are you doing with the clothes?"

"I'm pretty much done. But I don't know how to price them."

"I'll be up in about half an hour. And do me a favor? Try on one of the dresses so I'll have an idea of size."

"Right."

She returned to the upstairs bedroom.

The spirit of Clara? Nonsense! Sarah didn't believe in haunted houses. She turned on the overhead light, dispelling the shadows.

Some issues should be viewed clearly. Some decisions were etched in black and white. She needed to decide—right now—if she would make love with Mick. If she did, she could lose her job. At the very least, she could be horribly embarrassed by her inappropriate professional behavior. Those were the facts.

Added to that was another fact: Mick wasn't the sort of man who could make commitments. Though he'd said he wanted to be married, it was hard to picture him settled down.

He was a self-confessed loner. He didn't trust anybody. And without trust, there could never be real commitment.

Hard facts, she reminded herself. Black and white. Was an affair with Mick worth losing her job? Starting over on a new career track at age thirty-two?

But how could she say no? A man like Mick only came along once in a lifetime. He was tough and honest and brave.

Her gaze flicked around the old-fashioned bedroom. Clara might have shared that very bed with her violinist. Better to have loved and lost than never to have loved at all....

Sarah riffled through Clara's dresses and selected a pale blue chiffon dress to try on. Somehow, she wasn't surprised to find that Clara's dress fit perfectly. Even the matching stiletto-heeled shoes were the right size.

Sarah reluctantly stood in front of the full-length bedroom mirror and closed her eyes. Would she look as sophisticated as Clara, the opera singer? Or would the dress appear ridiculous?

Then she opened her eyes and stared at her reflection. Amazing. The everyday Sarah had vanished and an elegant lady had taken her place. Who said that clothes didn't make the woman? The gracefully draped neckline, nipped-in waist and flared at the hips made her slender figure appear as curvy as an hourglass.

When she heard Mick coming up the stairs, Sarah felt giddy as a teenager going to a high-school prom.

He came through the door, and she posed for him. The gleam in his eye was very satisfying.

"Beautiful," he pronounced.

"Isn't it? Approximately a size ten."

"I wasn't talking about the dress."

When he approached her, Sarah held out one hand to be kissed. Mick grasped her gloved fingertips, but his lips touched the bare skin at her wrist. "You look old-fashioned. Like that doll at the store."

"Is that a compliment?"

"I like the fantasy of the past. A porcelain princess," he said. "But that's not you, Sarah. You could never be that distant and untouchable."

She tilted her nose. "I could try."

"It'd never work. You're too much of a woman."

Her gloved hands stroked the T-shirt material on his chest, then glided around him.

His voice was husky. "You're too sexy."

"So are you. A handsome renegade." With his ponytail and his tough-guy attitude, he was the sort of man she could never bring home to mother—but Sarah's mother was in Florida. "I want you, Mick."

When he swept her into his arms this time, she knew there would be no turning back, no interruption. It was just Mick and herself and a four-poster bed.

His kiss overwhelmed her worries. Something that felt this good couldn't be wrong.

He caressed her throat, then pushed the blue chiffon down to bare her shoulders. The touch of his callused palms on her arms aroused her. He lowered the décolletage, revealing the blue unicorn he'd drawn upon her breast.

Sarah felt that her heart was beating so hard, the unicorn should dance. Her breast rose and fell with each breath she took.

"You've been careful to save this," he said.

"I needed the memento—to remind me that I could be wild."

Why the hell would she need to be reminded? He couldn't believe that Sarah was so unaware of her own sensuality. Sarah was very special. From the first moment he'd seen her, Mick had known that she was different from every other woman. And right for him.

He pulled the blue fabric of her dress lower, until it barely contained the fullness of her breasts.

"Should I take the dress off?" she whispered.

"*I* will, Sarah. In good time."

He eased one breast free of the dress. Her pink nipple was a tight little bud at the tip of her creamy flesh. And he needed to taste its sweetness. When he took her flesh into his mouth, he felt her shudder. She arched toward him. Her fingers tangled in his hair, tearing loose the rubber band that held his ponytail.

His hands slid down her waist and cupped her bottom. Then he stood and kissed her lips. Mick fitted her against his pelvis, feeling her softness against his erection. This was good. So good.

"I want you," she said again. "So much."

Reaching behind her back, he lowered the zipper of her dress and it slipped to the floor.

Sarah stepped out of her shoes. In bra and panties while he was still fully dressed, she felt vulnerable. "Now you," she commanded.

He peeled off his T-shirt, revealing his muscular chest which was nearly as tanned as his arms. The pattern of his black chest hair ended in a slender thread that disappeared into the waistband of his jeans. He was gorgeous. His virility was enhanced by his long, thick hair, and Sarah wondered why all men didn't choose to look like Samson.

Mick kicked off his sneakers. Then he unbuttoned his jeans. Before he stripped away his black bikini briefs, Sarah stopped his hands. "Let me," she murmured.

Quickly she stepped behind him and tugged them down. His flanks were tight and hard. And there, on his left cheek, she saw the tattoo. She touched the Monarch with wings spread. "You do have a butterfly on your butt."

"Very observant."

He turned and pulled her close. Hooking her thumbs in his briefs again, she exposed his penis, then pulled away the skimpy bit of material. Suddenly it occurred to her that she'd be a fool to make love without protection. "Mick? Do you have a condom?"

He nodded. "I'm not that much of a rebel."

He grabbed his jeans from the floor and dug into the pocket. While he sheathed himself, she tore away her bra and panties. Together they tumbled onto Clara's bed.

Sarah reveled in his touch. His rough hands teased her nipples and stroked her torso. "Soft," he murmured. "Your skin is like satin."

His mouth joined with hers, but his hands moved lower on her body. When his finger parted the delicate folds at the juncture of her thighs, she stiffened. But there was no chance of holding back; she spread her legs wide for him.

Her own fingers raced down his body, and she grasped his penis.

She was slick and ready.

"Now, Mick. Please."

His slow, deep thrusts drove her to the brink of frenzy. She writhed against him, breathing hard, and their lovemaking accelerated to a feverish pace. Faster. Faster. Shuddering, she allowed pure sensation to propel her into a most perfect orgasm.

Afterward, cradled in Mick's arms, she felt a wonderful glow. A glow, Sarah reminded herself, that could not be called love. Never love. Love meant trust. Love meant commitment. Oh God, what had she done?

Automatically her passion cooled, and she stiffened. She shouldn't have made love. It wasn't ethical business behavior. She imagined the Werner Foundation board of directors, pointing their accusing fingers at her.

Though she wanted to exist in the moment, that wasn't possible, and she slipped out of bed.

10

MICK WATCHED SARAH restlessly exploring the bedroom. The dim romantic lamplight made her look more enticing than ever.

"You've been possessed by the ghost of Clara," he teased.

She looked at him sharply. Sarah didn't want to share Clara's fate. She didn't want to be a woman who had waited and waited for the great love of her life...and then had lost him so quickly.

Feeling self-conscious because of Mick's intent gaze, she covered her breasts with her arm—a gesture that was hardly appropriate, considering their lovemaking.

As she stepped into the hall and headed toward the bathroom, Mick watched the gentle sway of her hips, then leaned back on the pillows. Usually, after sex, he felt energetic. He liked to get up and move around—to leave.

But he didn't feel like that with Sarah. Making love with her was different. He was satisfied, but not yet finished. He wanted to stay with her—and not just for the night. He wanted to stay with her . . . forever. He wanted to be with her, to laugh with her, to talk to her. She was honest, incapable of lying. When she meddled, it was because she really cared about other people. When she'd been afraid of riding on his motorcycle, her fear wasn't a coy trick. And when she kissed him, her desire was deep and true.

He could trust her.

Mick stared up at the ceiling. *Trust.* The concept of a woman he could trust was foreign to him. Not that he hadn't been involved with honest women. But real trust required the kind of commitment he'd never been able to give.

When his father's business collapsed, his family had needed for Mick to be a man. No more goofing around. And he'd shouldered their problems, taken on the responsibilities that his father couldn't handle. He'd been glad to do it.

But he knew there had been a price. Overnight, he'd had to stop being a wild college kid. In his early twenties, his own life had been put on hold. He'd had to bypass that stage when most guys figured out what they wanted to do with their lives and thought of settling down with a wife. Instead, Mick had jumped straight into adulthood, into a life where there didn't seem to be time for a mature relationship with a woman.

Or maybe he just hadn't met the right woman until now. Somehow, he sensed that he and Sarah were going to be great together.

Unfortunately, because he had to be at the flea market at dawn tomorrow, he needed sleep. They couldn't spend the whole night together. Not tonight. But there would be other nights. Many other nights.

She came back into the bed and snuggled up next to him.

This time, he touched her with less urgency. He smoothed the hair from her forehead and gazed into her beautiful brown eyes with their tiny flecks of gold. "You have beautiful eyes."

"They're just brown."

"Only at first glance. Then you look deeper, and you see these little gold sparkles." When he studied her face, he saw a loveliness that was sweeter because it was his alone. "Let me kiss your eyes."

She closed her eyelids and he lightly kissed them. She smelled so good, clean and feminine.

His lips sought her mouth, then he trailed kisses lower. It pleased him that she hadn't washed off his unicorn tattoo. And he tasted the flesh just below it. "Should we make this tattoo real? I know a guy who—"

"No," she said.

"It could be our secret."

"Not a chance. And you agree with me. That's why a rough, tough guy like you only has one teensy butterfly tattoo."

"You want me to get more?"

"Absolutely. How about a heart that says Sarah. With an arrow through the middle and blood dripping down. Lots of gore."

"And where should I have this tattoo?"

She allowed her gaze to caress his body. The sheet was casually tossed over his flanks, but his chest and arms were fully revealed. All muscle. How could she look at him without wanting him?

She touched his navel, then glided her fingers upward, twirling them in his chest hair.

"Mick," she said. "I'm worried about Lil."

Mick flopped back on his pillow.

"Worried about Lil?" he grumbled. "You've picked a fine time to be a social worker."

"The next time you see her, find out her last name and her phone number. All right?"

Mick didn't like the idea of invading Lil's privacy. But when he looked into Sarah's eyes, he couldn't refuse her request. "Okay, I'll do it. And I'll also ask around the neighborhood and find out if anybody's seen her."

"Thank you."

"We're real different," he said. "You and me, we don't think the same. But maybe that's what makes this—" he stroked her breast "—feel so nice."

"Maybe."

Sarah stretched the length of her body against his, then opened her thighs to encircle him. He was already hard, and she reveled in her power to arouse him. She kissed him with slow, self-indulgent languor. Her breasts tightened when she rubbed against the textured hair on his chest; she trembled when his hot breath touched her throat. He was so strong, so virile. And, for these few moments, he was hers alone.

Gazing fully into her eyes, he entered her. She arched against him and drew him deeper and deeper inside her.

Mick kissed her, the thrusts of his tongue matching the exquisite motion of his pelvis.

She murmured softly, wishing their lovemaking would never end. And yet, she was driven. Her body demanded climax. She slid against him, faster and faster until she could stand it no more. The spasms that racked her were incredible.

She couldn't believe that twice in one night, she'd found fulfillment. In the past, reaching orgasm had been difficult. But not with Mick. Sarah felt safe and warm and happy. "I wish we could stay like this all night."

"Me, too."

"But it's late, and we have to be up at dawn."

"I don't need sleep."

Yet, when she looked at him, his eyes were heavy-lidded. "I ought to be going," she whispered.

In a dreamy state, she crawled out of bed and dressed. She was glad that she had driven her own car to Clara's estate. Riding home on the back of his motorcycle would have destroyed her mood.

"Tomorrow," he said. "You'll be at the flea market."

"Yes."

"And tomorrow night. You'll be with me."

"Yes."

She kissed him again, then quietly walked to the door of Clara's bedroom. Long ago, the woman who had owned this house shared this very bed with her lover. Sarah prayed that her own passion with Mick would not come to such a premature end. When she turned and looked back at him, she saw the promise of many, many tomorrows in his eyes.

Sarah drove home, wanting nothing more than to crawl into her bed and lie there, savoring the memories of the most fantastic lovemaking she had ever experienced. She would never forget the texture of his long hair. Or the supple strength of his body.

When she parked in the driveway at her house, the first thing she noticed was that the living-room lights were still on. After eleven? Probably Jenny was still sorting her wares for the flea market tomorrow.

"Swell," Sarah muttered.

As she fitted the key in the lock, her sister yanked open the door. "I have something I need to discuss with you."

Sarah looked past Jenny's shoulder and saw two bearded men sitting at her dining table and laughing uproariously. "What's going on here? Who are they?"

"They're friends of Richard's from Australia."

"I see." Sarah calmed down. This was no big deal. Jenny's husband had sent good wishes to his wife and kids by way of a couple of his buddies.

She waved to the young men. They leaped to their feet and almost fell over each other in their enthusiasm to introduce themselves and shake her hand. Sarah was vaguely amused by their obvious interest in her. Weren't there any women in Australia?

She quickly excused herself and headed toward her bedroom, still clinging to the afterglow of her lovemaking with Mick.

At the doorway, Jenny stopped her. "Sarah, we need to talk."

"It's okay," she said. "Try not to make too much noise with Richard's friends. I'm going to bed."

But Jenny would not be dismissed. "Richard promised these guys that they could stay with me in Denver."

"Fine." A couple of student scientists spending the night would be okay. "They can help with the flea market tomorrow."

"For two weeks," Jenny said.

"What?"

"Please, Sarah. They spent all their money in Los Angeles, and they're broke and don't have anywhere to go. It's only two weeks, and I promise I'll take care of them. I'll do the extra cooking and cleaning."

"Two weeks is too long."

"But I can't throw them out. They're Richard's friends."

Sarah wheeled around, stormed into her bedroom and slammed the door. This intrusion was intolerable. Jenny's husband had offered Sarah's hospitality from across the globe. How could he have been so presumptuous? Sarah feared that her reputation as a sucker had spread to a worldwide level.

But this time, she wouldn't stand for the intrusion. There was a vast difference between being a decent, helpful sister and being a fool. She threw off her clothes, crawled into bed and turned off the light. Her anticipated sweet memories of Mick had fled before her head hit the pillow.

The next morning, before dawn, she avoided talking to the inconsiderate horde that occupied her home. She was outraged that the two student scientists were sprawled in sleeping bags in the middle of her living room. Dammit, this wasn't fair!

In fuming silence, Sarah took her place as the last car in the caravan driving to the flea market. Of course, she loved her family. Loved Charlie, even though his friend Tim was still living in the basement. Loved Jenny and Joey and Jamie. But this was too much.

At the flea market, they unloaded and set up Jenny's booth, which was inside the warehouse in an excellent location. Sarah was surprised at the number and variety of trinkets Jenny had managed to purchase with her three-hundred-dollar profit from last week. Had Jenny spent more? Was she risking her other savings on inventory?

One problem at a time. First, she planned to get Richard's friends out of her house. She pulled Jenny to one side. "Here's my decision, Jen. I want those two men out of my house by Monday."

"But Sarah, I can't—"

"Yes, you can. I'm not taking in these two strays, and that's final."

"I'll see what I can do. But when I came to live with you, the understanding was that your *casa* was my *casa*. I could treat your home as if it were my own."

Sarah winced, but held firm. "I'm sorry if I gave you the wrong impression. But I can't have any more people staying at the house. It's too much."

"All right. I'll try to get rid of them."

"And you'll pay for their food while they're here."

"Fine, Sarah. But you'll have to put it on my tab. I'm a little tight at the moment."

"Oh, Jenny. Tell me that you didn't spend your savings on this junk."

"That's my business."

When Jenny turned on her heel and stalked away, a very real concern surfaced in Sarah's mind. She might not be able to afford these extra houseguests. Sarah had always been prudent with her savings and investments, but what if she lost her job?

Frank Chapperal would be on her side, but Mr. Whelan was a difficult opponent. What if she were fired from the Werner Foundation? The economy was tight, and she had this great big house to maintain.

Maybe she should just dump the house and all earthly possessions and run away with Mick. They'd ride his motorcycle and live off the land like gypsies.

That fantasy faded as quickly as it had come. Sarah didn't want to live without a home, without knowing where her next meal was coming from. Despite the alleged wildness that Mick kept insisting was inside her, Sarah knew that her idea of being carefree was making a list with only three items on it. If she found herself unemployed . . . If more people moved in . . .

She looked up to see Joey and Jamie dragging Mick toward her. For a moment, the sight of them erased her worries. She was struck by the fact that Mick looked very natural with a small boy hanging from each hand.

"Here he is," Joey said, with the air of someone who had completed an important mission. "I found him."

"I did, too," Jamie put in.

"Thank you," Sarah said. "May I have him?"

Mick laughed. His smile—the comfortable smile from last night—was still in place. He looked down at Joey and Jamie. "Would you guys excuse us for a minute?"

"Okay. But you promised to take us to the playground."

"I think your mother could use some help," Sarah added.

The two little boys grumbled, but they obeyed.

When Mick took her hand, his touch sent a thrill from her fingertips, and though they stood in a crowd, Sarah felt as if they were alone.

"It's good to see you," he said.

"Same here. But . . ." She hesitated, her voice trailing off.

"Is something wrong, Sarah? What is it?"

"Other people." She told him about the houseguests. "I can't believe that Jenny's husband invited two of his friends to stay with me."

"I've got the perfect answer," Mick said. "Leave them all at your house and come live with me."

She didn't laugh. "I wish I could."

"Hey, Sarah, this isn't anything to worry about. Just kick them out. You don't have to take care of friends of friends and their second cousins."

"This is my sister we're talking about."

"Maybe not. It sounds to me like we're talking about you. You don't have to take care of the whole world."

"I know."

"But you can't help it, can you?" He gave her hand a squeeze. "Tell you what, Sarah. If you want to play Lady Bountiful, take care of me, okay?"

"What do you mean?"

His voice lowered. "Last night, you did a fine job of taking care of me. And you got something out of it, too."

"Yes," she whispered. "I did."

"That's what I want you to give. That's what I want to take." His tone lightened. "I mean it, Sarah. Put me on your permanent list. Write a memo."

"You've got it."

"Now, let's go find Joey and Jamie. Those two little guys have too much energy to be stuck with all these boring adults. They need a playground."

Joey was waiting for them at his mother's booth, but Jamie had wandered off and it took a couple of minutes chasing around the warehouse to find him beside a booth with stuffed animals. He stood mesmerized by a teddy bear that was as big as he was.

"Jamie," Sarah chided, "you mustn't go off by yourself."

"I like to explore," he replied.

"So do I," Mick said. "But sometimes that gets you into trouble. So, maybe it's a good idea to let your family know where you're going."

"Okay," Jamie said.

Though the boys were disappointed that Lil wasn't the caretaker at the playground, they recognized a few of the children from last week whom they greeted like long-lost friends. They waved goodbye to Mick and Sarah.

With her hand clasped in Mick's, Sarah strolled around the huge wooden warehouse. The sun had risen above the fields to the east. The dew had evaporated from the grasses, and the cloudless skies promised bright sunshine, a good day.

The gates to the flea market were open, and customers had already begun bartering and trading with merchants. She smiled at Mick. "Thanks for talking to Jamie. He does have a tendency to meander."

"I know how he feels. I'd like to meander away from here right now and take you with me."

"To a place where we could make passionate love?"

He lightly kissed her forehead. "Tonight."

She noticed a man coming toward them from the produce booths. He was Ray Innis from the Werner Foundation.

"Hello there," he called out.

"What are you doing here, Ray?"

"Aren't you going to introduce me to your friend?" He stuck out his hand. "I'll bet this is Michael Pennotti."

Mick shook his hand, but that was the only contact that Sarah intended for Mick to have with him.

"Please excuse us, Mick. I'll catch up with you later."

He hesitated.

"Please," she said.

Without saying a word to Ray Innis, Mick walked away.

Briskly, Sarah escorted Ray to a bench on the east side of the warehouse and sat down beside him. "What's going on, Ray?"

"I was instructed to come here and meet with Michael Pennotti."

"By Mr. Whelan?"

"He called me at home last night," Ray explained, with a smirk.

"I see. Did Whelan tell you that I was handling Mick's loan application?"

"He did. He explained that you were having problems convincing Pennotti to use his land as collateral for the loan." Another smirk. "Frankly, Sarah, after seeing you and Pennotti together, I can understand why."

"Did Mr. Whelan happen to mention that the signature on Mick's loan paper was forged?"

Ray's snickering expression disappeared.

"A forgery," she repeated. "Mick never actually applied to the Werner Foundation."

"Well, now, does it matter? Ask yourself that question. Does it matter that Pennotti didn't request the money? Whoever filed the application did him a favor. The board—according to Don Whelan—wants to give him money. A great deal of money at low interest."

"He doesn't want a loan. He adheres to the old-fashioned principle that money should be saved before it's spent. And nobody—not you or anybody else—can change his mind."

"I doubt that. The Werner Foundation wants to throw money at this guy. That's an offer he can't refuse. Nobody could."

"Mick could."

"Did you explain the loan completely?"

"Of course." But had she? Sarah thought back. Amazing as it seemed, with all the time and effort she'd devoted to Mick's loan package, they had never actually gotten down to the dollars-and-cents offer.

"I hate to say this, Sarah, but it seems to me that you're not objective about this project. Not when you're holding hands and playing kissy-face with the client."

She could have said that she'd held back as long as she possibly could. She could have told Ray that she and Mick had not made love until after he'd told her about the forgery and she'd dismissed his project. But Sarah knew there was no point in making excuses. Ray Innis was right. She had not behaved in a professional manner.

"You can't let your emotions get involved," he said. "I'm sure you agree with me on this."

"No, I don't. I am emotionally involved with almost all of my clients. I believe in their projects. I want them to succeed. I really hope that their projects will be good for the community, that their efforts might make a difference. That's why I work for a foundation instead of a bank."

Before Ray could get a word in edgewise, she continued, "But I am also a good businesswoman. I've been at this game for a long time, and I'm right about the way I've handled Mick Pennotti's loan." She played her trump card: "Frank Chapparel agrees with me."

"Chapparel? The former chairman of the board?"

"Frank was appalled. The forged application opens the possibility of a lawsuit. Not to mention the potential negative publicity." Her smile was condescending. "You're in a difficult situation, Ray. Though Mr. Whelan has requested that you pursue this project, you're flirting with illegality. Possible charges of harassment."

She allowed the words to sink in before adding, "If I were you, I wouldn't take further action until after the next board meeting. I believe it's scheduled for this Friday."

Ray didn't look happy about this turn of events, but he did seem convinced. "I'll see you on Monday morning, Sarah. Have a nice weekend." He stood and walked away.

A nice weekend? Despite her brave speech, her career was very probably in shambles. She had unwanted houseguests sleeping on her living-room floor. Her sister was mad at her.

What else could possibly go wrong?

11

SARAH SPENT ONLY a few fleeting moments with Mick the rest of the day. Which was just as well, because she felt guilty about not explaining the loan package completely. There was some truth in Ray's allegation that she hadn't done a thorough job. But how could she? From the first time she met Mick, there had been distractions. Maybe tonight they could discuss it. Ha! Discussion of loan prospects didn't exactly make appropriate pillow talk.

She picked up her nephews at the playground and took them exploring in the high grasses beyond the asphalt parking lot. Jamie wanted to catch a prairie dog, but—thank goodness!—the rodents were too fast.

Then Sarah followed Charlie around for a while, watching him interview merchants and shoppers for his projected doctoral dissertation.

It should have been an average day, a relaxing day. And yet, she felt haunted. Something was going to happen. Something awful.

Late in the afternoon, Sarah decided that she might as well confront her sister's hostility. It was better to argue here than at home with the two houseguests listening.

Inside the huge wooden warehouse, the crowds had thinned, and sales had slowed to a trickle. Jenny's booth stood out from the others in the row. Her painted plywood sign was written in flowing script, and the Tiffany lamp was classy and eye-catching.

"Hello, Jenny. How were your sales?" Sarah asked her.

"For your information, I've earned a gross profit of ninety-four dollars. Just for today."

"When you say gross profit, do you mean that you've earned back your investment in this merchandise?"

"I do. And I still have plenty of stuff left over for tomorrow. So there."

"I'm happy for you, Jen. You were right."

"I sure was! And you know what's the best thing about this? I can do this anywhere in the country. Maybe anywhere in the world. No matter where Richard goes for his research, I can work the flea markets."

"Sounds like you've found yourself a career."

"I have."

"Jen, I'm sorry we argued this morning."

"I'm not. It shows me where I stand with you."

A customer strolled into Jenny's area.

"I'll get the kids—I took them back to the playground," Sarah offered.

"Fine."

En route to fetch them, Sarah shuffled through the warehouse instead of going outdoors. Though the high-beamed building was still filled with merchants, business was slow. It was hot, and even the most avid of bargain hunters had given up for the day. A cleanup crew had already begun sweeping in the warehouse, raising a cloud of dry dust.

At the playground, she found Joey and Jamie, both of them tired and hot.

"Would a snow cone help?" she asked.

"You bet," said little Jamie.

"Not so fast," Joey told him. "Maybe we can make a deal."

Sarah laughed. "You've definitely been hanging around your mother's booth too long."

"If you buy us a snow cone, I'll give you one of my comic books."

"But, Joey, I would buy you a snow cone for free. You don't have to bribe me."

"But then, you're a sucker, Aunt Sarah."

"You bet I am. I've always been a sucker for a couple of handsome guys like you two."

"What about Mick?" Jamie asked. "Are you a sucker for him, too?"

"Maybe so." A knot tightened in the pit of her stomach. *A sucker for Mick?* "Maybe so."

When the boys had their snow cones, Sarah aimed in the direction of Jenny's booth. She paused at a display of vintage clothing to study the prices. None of the stylish old outfits was as well-preserved as the wardrobe she'd handled at Clara's house, but they were pretty. She took a lacy white blouse off the hanger and held it up.

"That would be lovely with a business suit," said the proprietor of the booth. "Looks like your size, too."

"Close enough," Sarah agreed.

"The blouse isn't all that old," the proprietor said. "If you dry-clean, it'll last for ages."

Mick appeared at Sarah's elbow and scrutinized the blouse. "We'll take it."

"Oh? Will we?"

"It's a present from me to you."

Instead of pleasant surprise, she was suspicious. What kind of present? Something for her hope chest? A thank-you? It wasn't her birthday. Second-guessing wasn't her game. If only things were more solid, more settled. "No, thank you," she heard herself say. "I don't want a gift."

But her words were barely audible over the roaring of a motorcycle engine from several booths away. Then a loud backfire erupted like a gunshot.

Sarah jumped. "What are they doing?"

"Being too loud," he replied. "Excuse me."

When Mick strode down the aisle, Sarah left the vintage-clothing booth to follow him. The grind of a second engine joined the first.

Mick stood beneath the sign that read: Cycles Custom. Sell And Repair. "Hey," he shouted. "I told you guys never to start those defective bikes in here."

A blond man with an Indian headband came to Mick. "How you doing, man? Still got that old Harley?"

"Yeah, I do. I love bikes. But you've got to take these cycles outside. You can't do repairs in here."

"Not repairs, man. We're selling these."

"You got a gas leak." Mick pointed to a puddle on the concrete floor. "Get those damn things out of here."

The revving of engines was deafening. Sarah covered her ears and watched Mick. His thumb jabbed toward the side exit. The other man shrugged.

Mick went to the first cycle and turned it off. As he approached the second, a third motorcycle sputtered to life. There was another booming backfire. Then a flare. A spark.

Sarah stared in horror as a bright flame caught on the gasoline that had leaked onto the floor of the booth. Suddenly a small fire danced wickedly around the motorcycles.

The machines were shut down, went silent, and their noise was replaced by the shouts of men who dived for cover.

Sarah saw Mick running toward the booth with a fire extinguisher in his hand. But he was too late. The flame hit the defective motorcycle. There was a dark burst, followed by an explosion.

Black smoke spewed outward, searing Sarah's nose and throat. She threw up her arm to protect her eyes. But still she saw the bright orange licks, and sparks that caught on every object they touched. The Cycle Custom sign was burning. The booth beside it, containing old furniture and draperies, ignited.

She heard screams, and the heavy smell of smoke clogged her nose.

Mick stood silhouetted against the spreading flames. He blasted foam from the extinguisher, but the fire leaped from one booth to the next. And onto the dry wooden wall of the warehouse. Too soon, his fire extinguisher was empty.

He flung the container aside and ran off.

"Mick!" she cried out.

She was afraid for him, knew that he was too brave for his own good. Her empty fingers clenched the hot smoky air, wanting to hold him back. But he disappeared. Sarah started in the direction he'd gone but a wave of heat drove her back. "Mick!"

Then she heard a cry, almost a whimper. Shielding her eyes, she looked toward the fiery space where the cycle booth had been. The bikes were charred hulks of metal, still burning.

Again she heard the whining cry. Something moved among the bikes. The blond man with the headband writhed on the concrete, trying to crawl. His singed T-shirt was plastered against his chest, greasy black soot streaked his flesh, and his left leg was twisted at an unnatural angle.

Fighting the heat, Sarah went to him, grasped his arms. With all her strength, she struggled to drag him. "Help me!" she called out. People were running all around them. "Somebody help!"

She was ten feet from the booth when another bike burst into flame. Any hope of containing the blaze was gone. Booths on the opposite side of the aisle were alight. Soon, Sarah would be surrounded with fire.

But she couldn't leave this injured man. He'd never make it out of the warehouse. Were there other injuries? What about the other men near the bikes? How many had there been? Four?

Suddenly she saw them. Four blackened figures. One of them bled from a gash on his arm. They staggered toward her.

"Take care of your friend," she ordered.

Fighting her way through the crowd, Sarah headed toward Jenny's booth. Her sister wasn't foolish, but Sarah feared that Jenny would disregard her own safety while she tried to move her merchandise, to save her brand-new career. Many of the other vendors were struggling to carry heavy loads.

At least Jamie and Joey were safe at the playground. She needn't worry about them. But then she saw two little boys. "Joey! Jamie!"

They were caught up in the crowd, headed in the same direction she was, but being swept farther and farther away from her. A wooden crate cracked against her shin, but she felt no pain as she propelled herself forward. She had to reach the boys.

Finally, frantically she clutched their small hands in hers. "Come with me."

"No, Aunt Sarah." Joey balked. "We've got to find Mom."

"Don't fight me!"

Meanwhile the fire had climbed upward, toward the high-beamed roof. The streams of water from cleanup hoses fought an impossible battle; they couldn't reach high enough. Soon, Sarah feared, the roof would collapse.

Pulling the boys, Sarah dashed for one of the warehouse exit doors. The doorways were huge, wide enough for a truck to enter, but their size provided an updraft that fanned the flames. Sarah shoved her way through to the outdoors.

Some distance away from the warehouse, she knelt on the asphalt of the parking lot. "You boys stay here. Don't go back into the warehouse, understand?"

"What about Mom?" Joey said.

Jamie started crying. "I want my mom."

"I'm going back in to get her," Sarah reassured them. "You stay out here. Understand?"

"Okay."

Fighting the crowd, Sarah wedged her way back inside the warehouse. The exits shouldn't have been so tightly jammed. The crowd should have emptied by now, but many were returning to rescue their merchandise. In and out. Back and forth.

Meanwhile the fire was spreading above the concrete floor, from booth to booth. It consumed old books and magazines. It devoured cardboard signs. And when she saw the flames racing up one side of the wooden warehouse, Sarah feared that soon the place would be an inferno. She found the booth where Jenny had been. All the merchandise was there, but Jenny had wisely fled.

The flames flickered closer and closer and Sarah knew she had to get out. Yet, through her fear, an anger burst. She would save something; she wouldn't allow this fire to destroy all her sister's hopes. She grabbed the valuable Tiffany glass lamp and followed the last of the people escaping through the wide doors. Sarah stumbled through the crowd holding on to the lamp and calling out her sister's name.

"I'm here, Sarah."

Jenny came up beside her. Her blond hair was coated with ashes. "The boys? Have you seen them? They're not with the others at the playground."

"They're out. I got them out."

"Thank God!" Jenny sobbed. "Help me find them, Sarah."

Together they scanned the groaning crowd. Some people had been overcome by smoke. Others wept silently. Sarah began asking, "Have you seen two little boys?"

"Joey!" his mother cried. "Jamie! Baby, where are you?"

Sarah saw a small blur and Joey raced up to his mother. He flung himself into her arms. Sarah felt partial relief, yet her grip on the Tiffany lamp tightened. "Where's your brother?"

"He's looking for Mommy, too."

"He didn't go back to the warehouse, did he? You didn't see him go there?"

"I don't think so."

Sarah set down the lamp and stared at the warehouse. Through the open doors, she could see the fire burning orange and brilliant. Could Jamie have gone back inside? He was only three years old. He didn't understand death, didn't understand that fire could kill.

This was her fault. Sarah should never have left the boys alone.

But maybe Jamie hadn't gone back inside. Maybe he was out here. Loudly, she announced, "Everyone listen to me. I'm looking for a three-year-old boy. Help me find him."

There was a murmur from the people near her. Sarah repeated her plea. And Jenny, through her sobs, echoed her words. The word passed from mouth to mouth.

"His name is Jamie!" Sarah yelled.

There were no cries of recognition. There was no relief.

Sarah turned back to the warehouse. It was better not to think about what she was doing. She rushed back toward the open doors.

"Look!" came a shout.

Through one of them, the figure of a man was visible against a wall of fire. Sarah knew without seeing clearly that the man was Mick. With a burst of speed, he charged into the sunlight. His body was greased with smoke. His shirt was seared and torn. In his arms, he held Jamie.

Sarah cleared a path, and Mick set Jamie down on a picnic table. He coughed, and in a tiny voice, said, "I want my mom."

"I'm here, baby." Jenny gathered him in her arms.

"I love you, Mom."

Jenny wept.

There was a loud crack from the warehouse as a portion of wall collapsed. Mick turned and stared at the huge old building. From the distance, he heard the sirens of fire trucks. Damn, it was about time!

He prayed that no one was still inside the building. He thought Jamie was the last. He hadn't seen anyone else. But if there'd been someone—even one person . . .

Every muscle in his body was taut with the need to do something. But there was nothing to be done. Not now. He was helpless against the force of the fire.

When he felt Sarah's arm around his waist, he held her tightly. Her face was smeared, and her shirt torn, but she was safe. She hadn't been hurt.

"It's going to be all right," she said.

"God, I hope so."

"Do you have insurance?"

"Yeah, and it's expensive as hell for a big wooden building." His itching eyes narrowed to slits as he peered at the flames. "Now I see why."

"I'm going to help you, Mick."

He glanced down sharply at the determined woman in his arms. What in hell was she talking about? Help him? Nobody could put out this fire. Nobody could help.

"Whether you want it or not," she said. "I have experience with situations similar to this, and I'm going to help."

Four ambulances pulled onto the asphalt parking lot, and the crowd shuffled toward them. Sarah climbed onto a picnic table. "Everyone please listen to me."

"And who the hell are you?"

"I am Mick Pennotti's associate."

"This is Sarah MacNeal." Mick jumped onto the bench beside her. He wasn't sure what she had in mind, but he trusted Sarah to do the right thing. "Do what she says."

"First, we'll take care of the injured." Remembering the blond man with the broken leg, she announced a plan. "I know there are people who are too badly injured to move. The ambulance personnel will come to them. Those who are hurt but able to walk, go to the ambulances."

"Hey!" shouted the woman who ran the burrito stand. "I still got cups, and there's water from the hoses. Anybody who wants a drink, come over here."

"Good," Sarah said. "Everybody who lost property or had property damaged, please see me at this table. I'll take your claims."

Astonishingly, there were only two serious injuries: the man with the broken leg, and an elderly man who was in shock. The rest of the injured had only suffered from minor burns, bruises and smoke inhalation.

With the entire warehouse burning like a dry torch, three fire trucks pulled up, and immediately radioed for more backup. Their primary concern was to contain the fire and prevent it from spreading onto the dry grasses of the surrounding landscape. Then the television-news trucks arrived. Eager reporters with microphones interviewed anyone who would talk with them.

In the midst of this hubbub, Sarah took names, addresses, phone numbers and estimates of loss. Jenny had fetched the briefcase from the trunk of her car, and Sarah filled one notebook after another.

By the time the sun had set, the fire had subsided to burning embers. Most of the people—including Jenny and the boys—had gone home.

Mick sat down at the picnic table beside her. "I guess this means our date is off," he said.

"Not necessarily," she replied. "Because you're coming home with me tonight."

"No, thanks."

"Don't be difficult, Mick." She felt like socking him on the jaw. Even if he was the toughest loner on earth, now was not the time to refuse care. "You can't stay here tonight. The fire hit your trailer. All the trees around it are burned."

"There's a bed in the back of Penny Wise."

"Forget it. You're coming to my house. And you're going to let Jenny make a fuss over you."

"I thought you already had a houseful of people."

"But you're an invited guest." He was, in fact, the only person she wanted to share her house with. "And I know exactly where I want you to sleep tonight."

"Okay." His eyes were bloodshot and tired. "Thanks, Sarah. You were a help."

She took his face in her hands and kissed him fervently. "Thank you, Mick," she said. "You rescued my nephew. I can never repay you for that."

He shrugged. "What else could I do? I saw the kid go running into the burning building, yelling for his mother. I couldn't just leave him inside."

"You're a good man, Mick Pennotti."

"And a tired one." He exhaled a long sigh. "I really messed up, Sarah. Big time. I never should have let those guys have a booth."

His face was smeared with soot. His hair frizzed in a singed mess, and his clothing was filthy and torn. Never before had he looked more like a renegade. But Sarah knew differently. Mick's instincts made him brave, true and admirable. Now, in Sarah's eyes, he would always be her hero.

12

SARAH'S TWO-STORY FRAME house seemed unusually quiet. When she opened the front door and shoved Mick inside before he could change his mind about staying, Charlie was the only one there to greet them.

Charlie went directly to Mick and hugged him. "Thanks, man. I should have been there, and I wasn't. I left early."

"Ignore him," Sarah said. "He's a psychology student so he hugs a lot."

"Not funny," Charlie replied.

She took a second look at her brother. His eyes looked bruised, as if he'd been crying. "You're upset, aren't you?"

"I knew it was too much for Jenny to handle this whole resale thing by herself. But I wanted to come home and watch baseball on the tube." His large hands balled into fists. "God, if anything had happened to Jamie, I would have blamed myself for the rest of my life."

"Nothing did," Mick said simply. He wasn't comfortable with praise when all he'd done was the obvious thing. "So why don't we forget it?"

"Where is everybody?" Sarah asked.

"Jenny and the kids went to bed. The students and Tim are out painting the town red."

"What are you doing at home?" Missing a chance to party? That wasn't like her brother. "Charlie, what's the matter?"

"I feel empty. There's nothing like a major trauma to put priorities in line. For the past few years, I've been screwing around, going to school and putting off doing anything responsible and grown-up. I don't want to be a kid all my life."

When she reached up to pat her brother's shoulder, Mick could see Sarah's exhaustion. He wanted to comfort her, to tell her that he appreciated the way she'd stepped in and helped, that he would forever be grateful to her. Grateful? Appreciated? He wished he could be as free with his emotions as Charlie was.

If Sarah hadn't stepped in when she did, the aftermath of the fire could have been a mob scene. Her composure had saved the day. But how could he tell her that he was proud of her?

Gruffly, Mick said, "Listen, Charlie, is there any food around here? All we've had for the past several hours were smoked burritos."

"There's enough food for an army. When Jenny came home, she fussed and cooked like mad. That's her way of dealing with things. But even Jenny couldn't keep up the front." He led them into the kitchen. "After the boys went to sleep, she collapsed on the sofa and cried her eyes out. I put her to bed."

The refrigerator was packed with slaw, potato salad, tuna salad and sliced ham. A feast.

"Help yourself," Sarah said. She sank down on a chair beside the kitchen table. "I'm not hungry."

Her brother dug into the freezer and produced a carton of chocolate ice cream. "This is for you."

"Very thoughtful." She nodded. "There's always room for chocolate."

Charlie dished her up a bowlful and said, "If you two don't mind, I'm going downstairs. I need to be alone."

"G'night, Charlie. Don't be too hard on yourself."

"I won't." There was a hint of bitterness in his voice. "I never am."

After Mick prepared some sandwiches, he sat down across from Sarah. Her eyelids were drooping and she'd dropped the spoon in the half-eaten ice cream. "Why don't you go to bed, Sarah?"

"I'm too tired." Her smile barely curved the corners of her lips.

"I'll carry you."

"No, thanks." With an effort, she hoisted herself to an erect posture. It was ironic, she thought. All day she'd been comforting herself with the idea of sleeping with Mick tonight. And now? "I'm going to wash off this dirt. My bedroom is on the far side of the living room."

"Will I be sleeping there?"

A faint light sparkled in her brown eyes. "Darn right."

When Sarah stumbled from the room, Mick sat there, thinking and eating. He heard the pipes rattle as Sarah started her shower. She was one helluva woman. Strong as steel. Mick felt lucky that she wanted him to stay here, that she wanted him at all.

He waited until he heard the water turn off, gave Sarah a few minutes to get settled, then went to do his own cleanup. The bathroom was down the hall from what had to be Sarah's bedroom.

Mick peeled off his clothes. God, he was filthy. When he washed himself, the water in the white tile shower stall bled gray. From the smoke, the fire.

He could still hear the crackle of dry wood, the roar of flames. But no one had died. The old man who'd been in shock had recovered. The cycle son of a bitch who'd started the whole thing had had his leg set and was already home from the hospital. No one was dead. But the destruction was complete.

When he crept into Sarah's bedroom with only a towel wrapped around his waist, Mick felt like an intruder in her feminine decor. The carpet was pale blue, the drapes white lace, and there was an ornate wooden dresser with a mirrored makeup table covered with an array of perfume bottles and cosmetics. In the double bed, beneath a fluffy white comforter sprigged with blue flowers was Sarah, fast asleep.

He closed the door and crawled into bed beside her. How could he wake her? She'd had one helluva day. But how could he not?

He rolled over and stared at her. Her hair was damp from the shower, and her bare arms were outside the comforter, but she wore a light cotton nightie with a low neckline.

"Sarah," he whispered.

She didn't even stir.

Surrounded by her presence, it was going to be impossible to sleep without making love to her. He closed his eyelids only to immediately envision the wall of flame that had destroyed his dreams, stripped him to the core. He'd never forget how helpless he'd been. This was how a disaster felt.

Mick thought of his father and his father's disaster. Long ago, when his father decided to move to Phoenix, Mick had helped with the packing. Among the last fragile things that went in the family car was a geranium planter. It wasn't anything special—just red flowers in an old china pot. But when Mick dropped it and the pot broke, he'd expected a tongue-lashing. He'd waited for the anger. Instead, he'd seen emptiness in his father's eyes. A broken pot didn't matter. Nothing mattered. His father had given up. The world had been too tough on him. Until now, Mick hadn't understood.

There were only so many times a man could be knocked down before he was knocked out. And what was he working toward, anyway? What was so god-damned important?

He hugged the pillow beneath his head. "Good night, Sarah."

Too quickly, nightmares overcame him.

THE NEXT MORNING, every bone in Sarah's body ached. And there was a heaviness in her chest. A pleasant heaviness, she realized. In sleep, Mick had thrown his arm across her.

She wriggled around in the bed to snuggle close to him. Despite the sore muscles and her bumps and bruises, she felt good, being held by Mick. And he was naked. Well, of course he was. She'd dragged him away from the fire with nothing but the clothes on his back.

Her fingers touched his cheek. His face was rough with stubble. But his hair, his beautiful long hair, was richly textured. And it smelled like her own shampoo. Though she ought to let him rest, she wanted to waken him with a kiss.

When his gray eyes opened, he said not a word. His mouth joined with hers. Gently, lazily, they kissed. Their bodies fitted more snugly together, sharing their sleepy warmth. His hand held her breast, and she could feel the nipple tighten in response to him.

From outside her bedroom, she heard the thumping of little feet. Jamie and Joey were up.

She smiled at Mick. "Did you sleep well?"

"A few nightmares." He squinted toward the window where the early-morning light filtered through her curtains. "It's still early. Why are we awake?"

"It must be my inner alarm clock. I'm accustomed to getting up early for work."

"You don't have to work today, Sarah."

The sensual message in his eyes was clear, and she was tempted to lock the door and forget about everything else. Just for one day, she could hide beneath the bedcovers with Mick. What a luxury!

Unfortunately, the moment she'd mentioned work, other matters slipped into her mind. "There's a board meeting on Friday," she said grimly. "I need to prepare."

She thought of smirking Ray Innis and Mr. Whelan's threat to fire her.

"Give it a rest, Sarah. It's Sunday. If God could take a day off when he was creating the universe, I bet the Werner Foundation can survive for a day without your help."

"Maybe you're right." She leaned across his chest and kissed him eagerly, savoring the thrill that went through her whole body.

"I *know* I'm right."

But she glanced at her clock radio: the digital numbers flashed seven thirty-seven. And just outside her bedroom door, she could hear Jamie and Joey, conversing in loud whispers. Sarah hauled herself from the bed, opened the door and glared. "Not now, boys."

"Hi, Auntie Sarah."

"Is Mick in there?"

"Can we come in?"

Sarah blocked their view of the bed. "You may not come in."

The two boys groaned. "I'll see you later, boys," Sarah said firmly and closed and locked the door.

Mick lay in the bed, chuckling.

"It's not funny," she said.

"Sure it is, *Auntie* Sarah."

She bounced into bed beside him. When she grabbed her pillow to throw it at him, her shoulder ached. Her entire body was stiff from yesterday's exertions. She wanted a back rub, wanted Mick to ease her soreness.

She wanted privacy, but that was not to be. She heard Jamie and Joey waking the students in the front room, and the rumble of their lower-pitched voices. The telephone rang.

Mick stroked the worry lines between her eyebrows. "This isn't like Clara's house."

"No, it's not." She would have given a lot to be alone with Mick.

There was a loud banging on the door. "Auntie Sarah! Telephone's for you."

With a sigh, Sarah lifted the receiver of the phone on her bedside table. "Hello?"

"Have you seen the morning papers?"

The voice was familiar, but . . . "Who is this, please?"

"Donald Whelan."

Sarah sat bolt upright on the bed. Donald Whelan? Calling her before eight o'clock on a Sunday? Couldn't he wait until the Friday board meeting to fire her?

"Your picture is on the front page of the *Denver Post*," he said. "At the fire. What the hell happened?"

"It was an accident. Mick Pennotti's flea market burned to the ground. His trailer was also destroyed. Fortunately, the fire department arrived in time to contain the blaze and prevent a brushfire from developing."

"Good."

"Why are you calling me, sir?"

"I was concerned about your safety."

"Really?" She found that very hard to believe.

"And I wish to propose a compromise on this Pennotti situation."

Undoubtedly, she thought, he had spoken with Ray Innis. Her heart sank with a thud. Did Whelan know about her relationship with Mick? "A compromise?"

"It has come to my attention, Sarah, that your handling of this 'affair' has been less than professional. I understand that you've become personally involved with Michael Pennotti."

Sarah glanced over at the bed where Mick lay watching her. Personally involved? That was an understatement.

"Furthermore," he continued, "you're attempting to use your relationship with Frank Chapparel to make me look bad with the other members of the board."

"I'm not trying to make you look bad. I'm simply telling the truth."

"But the truth isn't in your best interests. If the rest of the board learned how 'involved' you've become with this particular client, you would not only be dismissed from the Werner Foundation, but you might find it difficult to get another job. That's a nasty stain on your record. Isn't it, Sarah?"

Very nasty. And very deep. She sighed. "What sort of compromise are you suggesting?"

"You hand over your files to Ray Innis. You call Frank Chapparel and tell him that you must have been mistaken about the forgery. Then you erase it from your mind. Speak to no one about it. Refer all inquiries to Ray. In exchange, I won't mention your indiscretion."

It was blackmail. Pure and simple. But did she have another choice? "I'll think about it."

"Not good enough, Sarah. I want your silence. And I want it now. You're not to talk about this situation to anyone. Especially not to Michael Pennotti."

She could feel Mick's presence on the bed behind her. His warmth. If she turned slightly, she would see him. She could stretch out her hand and touch him. With very little encouragement, he would make love to her. How could she promise not to be completely open with him?

"Do we have a deal, Sarah?"

What choice did she have? "Yes."

"Good. Very good."

She could hear the triumph in his voice, and she hated it. She hated Whelan. And hated herself for agreeing to blackmail.

"This morning, Sarah, at ten o'clock—"

"But it's Sunday."

"This morning, you will meet Ray Innis at your office. And you will hand over the files."

"I'll be there."

She slammed the telephone back onto the receiver. Her job wasn't worth it. She'd find something else. Whelan was wrong when he said no one else would hire her. Denver was a big city. And she was a capable administrator. She could start over with a company that didn't need to know about her "indiscretion."

When Mick touched her shoulder, she jumped.

"What's wrong?" he asked. "Bad news?"

"I'm going to the office. Something came up."

"What is it, Sarah? You can tell me."

"I have to get dressed."

She rose from the bed. Without looking back at him, she went to the closet and found her bathrobe and thrust her arms into the sleeves. How could she be less than completely honest with Mick? He had just begun to trust her, to believe in her.

"Sarah."

Before she tightened the sash on her robe, Sarah slowly turned around and looked at him. His expression was serious, full of compassion.

She smiled nervously.

When he smiled back at her, her heart ached. She didn't deserve one of his infrequent smiles.

"Come here, Sarah."

Woodenly, she went to the bed and perched on the edge. He opened the front of her robe. His hands glided down her arms, grazing her breasts. Her nightie felt flimsy and insubstantial.

"It's gone," he said.

What was gone? She started. Her honor? How could it be so obvious? Had she sprouted a big red *L* for *Liar* on her chest? "What's gone?"

He pointed to a spot above her left breast. "The unicorn. You must have washed it away in the shower last night."

The faint outline of his handiwork was barely visible. The color had faded to a shadow.

Unthinkingly, she had erased the unicorn tattoo. But she wouldn't allow her relationship with Mick to fade. Nor would she give in to Whelan's blackmail. Sarah rose to her feet and tightened the sash of her robe. "I need some time, Mick. There are a few things I need to straighten out in my mind."

"Tell me about that phone call."

Despite her resolve, she looked him directly in the eye and told her first lie. "It was nothing important. Nothing at all."

13

SARAH HATED the sticky, sour taste of lying. And she hated herself for being scared away from the truth. This web could ensnare her. It could end with Mick despising her. But what else could she do?

Angry and confused, she stormed around the kitchen, brewed coffee and threw together a breakfast of cereal for the boys. And tried to think. She needed a list. But what would it say? "1. Get blackmailed. 2. Lose your job. 3. Be dishonest."

She went to the counter to watch the coffee drip through the machine. How could she lie to Mick? When she'd awakened this morning, cocooned in her bed beside him, the moment had been so peaceful. When he'd touched her and kissed her—whenever he kissed her— her pleasure was intense. All because he'd learned to trust her. How could she jeopardize that fragile trust?

Still, she decided not to tell Mick about the threat to her job. Not because of Whelan's insistence that she shouldn't, but because Mick had enough to worry about—the fire, the theft, running his business.

She desperately needed a battle plan.

What next? Sarah had promised to meet with Ray Innis in two hours, to hand over Mick's file and to talk with Frank Chapperal. Talk with Frank? That telephone call might be the answer to Whelan's blackmail. Though Whelan expected her to meekly apologize and withdraw her accusation of forgery, Sarah had another option. She could call upon Frank Chapperal for support.

Her hand was on the receiver of the kitchen phone extension before she remembered that it was only eight o'clock on a Sunday morning. A bit early to be calling the former chairman of the board. She'd give him half an hour. Then . . . what would she say?

Joey came bouncing into the kitchen. "Aunt Sarah, Mick says he doesn't have any clothes to put on."

Despite her mountain of worries, Sarah laughed. Though she liked the idea of keeping Mick barefoot and naked in her bedroom, he surely wouldn't go along with it. "Joey, why don't you run downstairs and ask your Uncle Charlie for some clothes for Mick?"

Two minutes later, Jamie dawdled over to her and hugged her leg. "I was supposed to tell you something."

"About Mick?"

"Yep. He says you better hurry up."

"You tell him to keep his shirt on."

"But he hasn't got a shirt." Jamie brightened. "I can give him mine."

The two bleary-eyed students came into the kitchen, followed by Jenny who immediately began organizing a huge breakfast. Joey streaked past with clothes for Mick.

Sarah poured a mug of coffee for herself and one for Mick, then retreated to her bedroom. She opened the door just in time to see Mick pull on a pair of her brother's pants. Sweatpants. Baggy gray. With matching sweatshirt.

"I hate these," he said. "Feels like I'm wearing pajamas."

"They're cute." She handed him coffee. "But I liked you better without them."

"What did you mean by marching off and leaving me here naked?" He slurped the black coffee. "That phone call upset you. And I want to know why."

"It's about work." That was true. "I have to report in to the office, and I don't want to." Also true.

"On the phone, you started off talking about the fire at the flea market. You called it Pennotti's flea market. Does this work you're doing today have anything to do with me?"

Sarah had never been good at lying. Anytime she veered away from the truth, her lips quivered. Hoping to cover, she held her coffee mug in front of her mouth. "The fire. Well, you see, Mick, my photograph is on the front page of the *Post*. I'm going to get a lot of calls about that."

"Front page, eh?" His gray eyes narrowed, and she cursed his talent for reading people. It felt as if he could see right through her. "Are you sure that's all?"

"Yes." She changed the subject. "Why don't you have some breakfast?" she suggested. "I have to get ready."

When she pulled open the bedroom door, Jamie and Joey tumbled inside. Obviously they'd been listening at the keyhole.

"Are you going to kiss her?" Joey asked Mick.

"Think I should?"

"Yeah."

"Okay, boys, this is how you do it." Mick took the coffee mug from her hand and set it on the bedside table beside his own. "You've got to move fast so she can't tell you no."

He placed his hands at her waist and quickly pulled her toward him. Knowing that they were being avidly observed by Joey, who had apparently reached the age where he was curious about girls, Mick restricted himself to a chaste kiss on the lips.

"Excellent," Joey said.

Acknowledging the compliment, Mick bowed from the waist. "And that, my boy, is how it's done."

"What is this?" Sarah grumbled. "A training program for male chauvinist piglets?"

"I'm not a piglet," Jamie protested.

Mick explained, "Joey wanted to know if I liked you—even if you are a girl. And I told him that being a girl was one of the nicest things about you. Then I said I'd show him why."

"How adorable." Sarah pushed Mick toward the boys. "Feed this oinker, okay?"

The two boys pulled Mick from the room, and Sarah closed the door. She sat on the edge of the bed and dialed the home phone number of Frank Chapperal.

AT QUARTER TO TEN, Sarah drove into the underground parking garage of the downtown tower where the Werner Foundation's offices were located. Since she frequently worked on weekends, the ritual for entering the building after hours was familiar—she rode the elevator to the fourteenth floor.

The lights were already on. Ray Innis must have arrived early. How typical, she thought. Eager Ray had come here in hot pursuit of career advancement. She found him standing outside her office, neatly dressed in a blue serge suit and reading the *Wall Street Journal*. He looked up. "I'm sorry, Sarah."

Not half as sorry as he was going to be. Her smile was cold. "Please come with me."

"Wait a minute." He balked. "I want you to know that my apology is sincere. I didn't expect Whelan to react the way he did. Has he got some kind of personal vendetta against you?"

"He doesn't like me because I'm standing in his way. That's all. I have nothing more to say right now, Ray."

She marched into her office and pulled Mick's file, but she didn't give it to Ray. Instead, she directed Ray back to the elevators. The boardroom was one floor up, and Frank Chapperal had agreed to meet them there. Sarah hoped he had arrived on time.

"What's this about?" Ray demanded.

"You'll see."

In the paneled boardroom with its panoramic view of the snow-capped Rocky Mountains, Frank Chapperal sat at the head of the long, gleaming oak table. In contrast to Ray's neat suit, Frank wore casual slacks and an open-necked cotton shirt. Though his appearance was youthful and vigorous, Sarah noticed strands of gray in his thick red hair.

"Good morning, Sarah. Ray."

He rose to shake their hands, motioned for them to sit, then turned his wrist to glance at his watch. "I'll be brief. I was glad when Sarah telephoned this morning because I've obtained new information on the forged loan application."

"Forged?" Ray questioned. "I don't mean to be rude, but are you certain that Mr. Pennotti's application was forged?"

"Very certain. In fact, I know who filled out the form."

Sarah sat up straighter in her chair. "Who?"

"I'd rather not say. But I assure you that this person had the best intentions. There were no nefarious motives involved. Only a misguided desire to help."

He frowned, and Sarah noted real concern in his expression. Why? Who could have provoked this reaction? Certainly not Whelan. But if Whelan hadn't forged the application, who had?

"The individual involved will be dealt with." He turned to Ray. "However, I insist that the file be closed. It's lucky for us that Sarah convinced Pennotti not to sue the foundation."

Ray nodded obediently, but added, "Don Whelan has taken a strong interest in this project. He'll be disappointed."

"Let me deal with Don," Frank said grimly. He rose to his feet. Both Sarah and Ray did the same. "That will be all, Ray. I'll see you at the board meeting on Friday."

"Thank you, Frank."

When Sarah stood and prepared to follow Ray from the boardroom, Frank said quietly, "I'd like another minute of your time, Sarah."

While she fidgeted in her chair, waiting for Ray to leave the room, her anticipation grew. Finally she was going to find out who committed the forgery.

Frank spoke slowly, almost painfully. "I'm disappointed in you, Sarah. There's something going on between you and Mick Pennotti, isn't there?"

She nodded. It took all her willpower not to cringe. "I assume you've spoken to Mr. Whelan."

"Actually, I haven't."

"Then who?"

"Sarah, your behavior on this project has been far below your usual standards. If Whelan pushes for your dismissal, I'm not sure that I can stop him."

"I understand." She was going to be fired. She was going to lose. "But I won't resign. My relationship with Mick might be imprudent, but it isn't wrong."

"You're going to contest it?"

"Yes." Her resolve held firm. "And I need your help. Tell me who committed the forgery. Was it Whelan?"

"No." Frank pushed away from the table. With heavy steps, he went to the windows and stared out with hands clasped behind his back. "The person who filled out Mick's application went through his desk at Penny Wise to obtain the figures, then forged his signature. This person broke the law and must be taught that there are consequences for such behavior."

When he faced Sarah, she saw the beginnings of a smile on his face. "Yet, the actions of this person, this forger, were based on a desire to help Mick finance his dream. In some ways, her behavior was commendable."

"*Her* behavior?" It was a woman?

"It was my daughter, Caroline. I believe you know her."

Sarah shook her head. His daughter?

"Caroline has red hair, like mine. She's sixteen. And she has a godawful lily tattoo on her shoulder."

Lil. Mick had told her that Lil wasn't her real name, but a nickname he'd given her because of the lily tattoo. Caroline Chapperal was Lil?

Stunned, Sarah fell back in her chair. Yet, his explanation made perfect sense. Lil had easy access to Mick's files. Lil wanted to help. And Lil must have been the one who had informed her father about Sarah's involvement with Mick. "Your daughter?"

"After you called and mentioned Penny Wise, I remembered that Caroline liked that shop. I thought she might be involved in this, but I never expected her to do something like forging a loan app." His wry smile widened. "I wish she'd apply the same creativity and energy to her schoolwork."

"She's a surprising young woman." Sarah wondered if Lil, alias Caroline, had told her father that she'd witnessed a robbery at Penny Wise. Probably not. And this was probably not the best time to mention it.

"I feel like I'm somehow closer to Caroline because of this," Frank mused. "She only lives with me part-time because of the divorce, and I never thought she gave two hoots about my work, but the girl must have been paying attention. It must have clicked in her mind that the Werner Foundation likes to fund projects that help the community."

"Maybe she has a future in business."

"Maybe." He pivoted and stared directly at Sarah. "In any case, we need to make this mess go away. I've instructed my daughter to find Mick Pennotti, today, and to tell him what she did. If he's half the man Caroline thinks he is, he won't take advantage of my wealth to press charges against my daughter."

Mick? Take advantage? Sarah knew that wasn't part of his nature. "I can almost promise you that he won't."

"Do you happen to know how or where she can reach Mick?"

"He's staying at my house."

"Your house?" Frank's eyebrows raised. "This relationship you have with Mick is more than an indiscretion. Do you love him, Sarah?"

Did she? She was certainly putting a great deal at risk if she didn't. And yet, she wasn't sure if she'd call it love. He hadn't given her hearts and flowers. Their only real "date" had been a spaghetti dinner at his trailer.

She loved being with him, loved his elusive smile, loved making love with him. But *in* love? "I don't know."

THE FIRST THING Mick did upon entering Penny Wise that evening with Sarah was to turn on the cooling system. There was no air-conditioning in the old building, but the circulating fans stirred life into the warm, stale air.

Mick had been surprised when Lil telephoned him earlier in the day to set up a meeting time. But he was glad. He was going to need every nickel to clean up after the fire and the theft, and if Lil had decided to come forward as a witness, it would look good with his insurance company.

In his office, Mick searched for the appropriate ledgers and bank statements to copy for his insurance agent. Luckily he hadn't lost the paperwork from his trailer. He'd picked it up today when Charlie drove him out to the flea market. The *former* flea market, he mentally corrected himself. It looked like hell out there. Rubble and scorched two-by-fours were all that was left of the warehouse. His trailer was still standing, but the fire had wiped out his water and electric system, making it impossible to live there. Fortunately his clothes and papers were intact—stinking of smoke, but intact. And, ironically, his Harley ran.

It would take work, but he could survive this. He had Penny Wise, the estate sale at Clara's house had earned a tidy profit, and he owned his land. Though Mick would have been crazy to be cheerful after these disasters, he wasn't feeling down.

Right now, the thing that bothered him most was Sarah's behavior. There was something weird about her. After that phone call this morning, she'd been evasive. Her gaze kept sliding away from his. Whenever he asked her about the call, her lips began to tremble.

He stood in the door to his office and watched her browse through Penny Wise. She was admiring that porcelain doll again. "Are you ever going to tell me?" he asked.

When she looked up, her eyes were wide, but as glassy as the eyeballs of the doll. He knew she was hiding something.

"Tell you about what?"

"The phone call."

"It was only business."

"Dammit, Sarah." Mick turned and went back into his office, convinced that she was lying to him.

"I'm sorry," she whispered, as she fought the urge to confess. Lil would be here soon. Soon enough, Mick would understand.

Sarah hugged the doll. It seemed impossible that only a few weeks ago, she'd entered Penny Wise for the first time. Now the jumble of merchandise seemed like old friends. The rocking horse was gone. But there was a new display of lamps. Some of Clara's vintage clothing had found its way into the racks.

This was part of her life now. She placed the doll back on the shelf and smoothed the tattered velvet gown.

Just then, Lil slinked through the back door and glared at her.

"Mick?" Lil shouted.

He poked his head through the office door. "How are you doing, Lil?"

"What's Sarah doing here? I wanted to see you alone."

"You can trust her," Mick said. "She's not going to do anything to hurt you."

"That's not what Lil means." Remembering Lil's crush on Mick, Sarah understood the hurt in the girl's eyes, the pain of being rejected. "You two have a relationship that I'm not part of, and I respect that. I'll leave you alone to talk."

But when she turned to leave, Lil darted over to her and caught her arm. "You really messed things up for me, Sarah. I was trying to help, and now everybody's mad at me."

"You did this yourself." Sarah kept her voice low so Mick wouldn't hear. "I know you're only sixteen, but surely you realized from the start that forgery was wrong."

"So what? If Mick had taken the money and started on his warehouse project, everything would have been fine. I would have told him—someday."

"You still have a chance to help him," Sarah said. "His insurance company suspects that the robbery here wasn't real. A witness, like you, might make a difference."

"What? I didn't come here to talk about that."

"If you care about him—"

"Don't talk to me about caring, okay?" Her wiry body tensed. "You don't know what it's like for me. If I talk to the cops, my dad is going to be so mad. He'll probably kick me out of the house."

"Don't underestimate your father." Softly, Sarah added, "He cares a lot about you, Caroline."

"Hey!" Mick called to them. "What are you two talking about? I thought Lil came to see me."

"I did." In a lightning-quick teenage mood change, her eyes softened. She looked frightened, hurt. "What am I going to do? Sarah, what should I tell him?"

"The truth."

Good advice, Sarah thought. If only she could follow it herself.

14

MICK SAT BEHIND the desk in his office. "Sit down, Lil."

After a moment's stubborn hesitation, she plopped down on the wooden chair opposite his desk. "I'm sitting."

"What were you and Sarah talking about?"

"She makes me so mad. All that goody-goody stuff. She's going to get what she deserves and I'm going to be glad."

Mick had never seen this side of Lil's character before. She'd always been sweet—strange, but sweet. Her vehemence shocked him. "What does Sarah deserve to get?"

"She's going to lose her precious job, that's what. And I hope she can't find another one." Lil's lip quivered. "I hope she ends up on the street, rotting like an old tomato."

Completely confused, Mick leaned back in his chair, distancing himself from this strange outburst. What did Lil know about Sarah's job?

"It's all her fault, Mick. Don't you see? If she'd just put through the loan without talking to you in person, nobody would have known about the forgery. You would have gotten your money and you could build your warehouses and—"

"Hold it!" Mick was beginning to get the picture. "How do you know about the forgery?"

"Because I did it." Lil jolted to her feet. "Okay? I'm a terrible person because I filled out some stupid form."

She stormed across the office. Her tiny fist smacked loudly into a file cabinet, and she winced with pain. "Ow! Everything is against me. This isn't fair."

While she ranted, Mick stared. Lil had filled out the form? Lil? This kid with a lily tattoo? Mick wouldn't have expected her to know how to keep a bank balance in a checkbook, much less to fill out a complicated loan application.

"You're all picking on me!" Lil shouted.

"I'm going to do more than pick," Mick warned. "You sit your butt down in that chair, young lady. I'm not in the mood for your temper tantrum."

She stiffened. "Don't treat me like a baby."

"Then stop acting like one."

Cradling her injured hand against her chest, she sat, looking as though she was either going to burst into tears or throw something at him. "Tell me the whole story, Lil."

"My name's not Lil. It's Caroline. Caroline Chapperal. My father is on the board at the Werner Foundation."

"Wait." Mick held up his hand. He looked at the baggy shirt she wore, and the torn cutoff jeans. On her feet, he knew, were black high-top sneakers. "Your family is wealthy?"

"Money doesn't matter to me. Anyway, my dad is always blabbing about the foundation and how they help people to help themselves. That's supposed to be a lesson for me. I'm supposed to help myself to be a better person."

Mentally, Mick filled in the blanks. Lil—or Caroline—had swiped a loan app from her father, then she'd come into his office at Penny Wise, probably on the pretext of typing a paper for school. She'd gone through his files and filled in the blanks. Then she'd signed his name to it. "Why?"

"I wanted to do something for you. You've been so nice to me, treated me like I was a real person, like I could understand things. And when you talked about your warehouse project, your eyes got kind of dreamy. I knew you wanted it. Wanted it bad. And I thought I could help."

Her thin voice caught in a sob, but Mick had no sympathy for Lil. Or Caroline. Or whatever her name was. He hated lies and liars. Her youth was no excuse. Nor were her intentions.

"Are you mad?" she asked.

"Damn right."

"But it's not like I really lied to you. I just kind of didn't mention things. And it would have turned out fine if—"

"That's why you couldn't go to the cops about the robbery, isn't it? Because you're not Lil. You're Caroline. A spoiled brat who doesn't want to make her daddy mad at her."

"I don't care about him."

"Maybe you should. From what you've said, he doesn't sound like a bad guy. Is he the one who told you to come down here and confess to me?"

"Yes," she whimpered.

"What would he say if he knew you'd witnessed a robbery?"

"First he'd be mad at me for sneaking out of the house and hanging around in a bad neighborhood at night."

"Then what?"

"He'd tell me to go to the police," she admitted.

"I agree with your father," he said. "Do it."

Tomorrow or the next day, he might be able to forgive Lil, but right now he was too damn mad. He had trusted this girl, had allowed her access to his office, had encouraged her to play the piano. He'd even found a secondhand electronic keyboard for her to buy. "Did you steal the keyboard?"

She nodded. "When I came back into the store after the thieves left, it was just sitting there. I wanted it." She slouched down in her chair and muttered, "You said I should go after the things I wanted."

"I didn't mean you should steal." Mick sighed with frustration. "Okay, Lil—I mean, Caroline. So far you've stolen from me, lied to me and forged my name. Is there anything else? What was the stuff you said earlier about Sarah's job? Another lie?"

"No," she shot back. "She's the one who started this. She called my father and told him about the forgery. And then he talked to me because he knew I hang out at Penny Wise. After I told him about the loan application, I told him that Sarah was messing around with you."

"You did what?"

"It's the truth," she said.

Mick couldn't argue with that. But he also realized the implications in a business sense. Sarah had been "messing around" with a potential loan applicant. She could lose her job because of him. That must have been what the phone call this morning was about. She should have told him. Was Sarah, like Lil, not really lying, but not telling him everything?

"I'm sorry, Mick. Is there anything I can do to make it better between us?"

"You can get out of here and leave me alone."

He heard the wooden chair squeak on the floor-
boards, heard her ragged breathing, heard her walking
heavily toward the door. Mick looked up. "Lil."

Eagerly she turned. "Yes?"

"I'll calm down in a couple of days. And we can be
friends again. But right now, I'm still teed off."

"Whatever you say, Mick. And I'll go to the police
station tomorrow and make a report. Okay?"

"Whatever."

"Mick? Are you in love with Sarah?"

He had thought that he was. There'd been moments.
Like last night when he'd watched her sleeping. And at
Clara's house when she was showing off the blue dress.
And last week at the flea market when she stepped out
into the rain and allowed it to run down her cheeks and
through her neat hair. He remembered watching her face
while he drew the unicorn on her creamy breast.

But the unicorn was gone. Erased. And there couldn't
be love without trust. "That's none of your business, Lil."

She grinned. "I'm glad you're still calling me Lil.
Maybe I'll get my name changed legally."

"Fine. Great. Wonderful. Just don't do anything to
help me again."

"Okay." With a resilient smile, she left his office.

He leaned back in his chair and waited for Sarah to
enter. She had some explaining to do, but Mick wasn't
sure he wanted to hear her answers. Like Lil, she hadn't
actually lied to him, but she hadn't told him everything,
and Mick wasn't sure how that made him feel. With Lil,
the deception had been an infuriating annoyance. But
with Sarah...

The matter of trust between them was far more important. He didn't want to look at her and wonder if she
was telling the truth.

Moments later, she appeared at his office door. Ignoring the wooden "interrogation chair" opposite the desk, she leaned against the door frame and stood there, meeting his gaze.

The difference between Sarah and Lil was striking. Sarah was a mature woman, dressed neatly in a cotton skirt and blouse. With her, there would be no nonsense. No tantrums. She looked cool and poised—and sexy as hell.

"I guess Lil told you about the forgery," she said. "I knew about it this morning, but I kept it from you. I wanted her to be able to make the confession herself."

"You lied to me."

She didn't make excuses, didn't deny her guilt. Instead, she confronted him directly. "Yes."

"Lil also said that you might lose your job because of our relationship."

"That's true. Sleeping with potential clients is considered unacceptable behavior." A smile tugged at her lips. "That's kind of an understatement."

"What are we going to do about it?"

"There's a board meeting on Friday of this week. Either I'll be given a reprimand, or I'll be fired. At this point the decision is up to the board, and there's nothing I can do."

"You could deny it," he said. "I know your job is important to you. If you wanted me to lie for you, I'd do it."

Sarah couldn't believe she'd heard him correctly. Mick was as honest as the day was long. And he was offering to lie for her. The prospect was tempting but impossible. Ray Innis had seen her with Mick. Lil could corroborate. And she didn't want to start a cycle of name-calling. "I don't want you to lie. I've hated not being able to tell you the whole truth today, and I don't want any more deception."

"I'm glad."

He came out from behind his desk and crossed the tiny office in two strides. Now that the deceit between them had vanished, her gaze was clear-eyed. "Is there anything else you haven't told me about?"

She shook her head. "Lil was the forger. And I might be fired. It's more sordid and complicated than that, but essentially those are the facts."

Sarah wrapped her arms around his neck and pulled him close. More than anything, she wanted to show him exactly what her lips were made to do. Their kiss was slow, sensual.

It had only been a few days, a brief time that could be measured in hours, since they'd made love at Clara's house. But it felt like a hundred years. She never wanted to be apart from him again.

His hands stroked her breasts, and she felt the incredible stirrings that only Mick could arouse. Her breath came in rapid gasps. She wanted to make love, right here on the hardwood floor of his office. "Is there a bed in here?"

"It's not put together."

"Oh." But she wanted to make love to him, now. "How long would it take to—"

"Longer than I can wait."

Swiftly, his fingers unfastened the buttons on her blouse, pulling the flimsy cotton material loose from her skirt and tossing it aside. He tugged at her bra, and Sarah reached up to unfasten the snaps, freeing her breasts. He kissed her again with hard urgency. She wanted him so much, wanted the truth of their lovemaking to supplant the ugly taint of lies.

When her hands slid below his waist, cupping his erection, he turned her, lifting her so that she was sitting on his desk. He lowered his mouth to her breasts and sucked her nipples, teased the sensitive peaks with flicks of his tongue.

Her teeth gritted against the force of her rising passion. "I want you, Mick. I want you inside of me."

Sliding his hands up her leg, he pulled off her panties, then unfastened his jeans.

With eager intensity, Sarah spread her thighs. Her skirt bunched up around her waist. Driven by passion, she pulled him against her, encircled him tightly with her legs. She clung to him, dragging him with her onto the desktop, scattering the papers he'd gathered for the insurance company.

Mick poised himself above her, and she saw the fierce need in his eyes—a need mirrored in her own tense expression. Then he plunged into her, thrusting deep and hard.

Her desire for him was greater than her logic, greater than her awareness of her surroundings. There was only Mick, his body, and the throbbing rhythm of their lovemaking.

Her heart fluttered. She reached climax and gasped as he, too, spent his passion inside her.

Gently her mind drifted back to awareness. She saw the fluorescent lights overhead, felt the hard surface of the desk beneath her. "I don't believe I just did this."

He stood and refastened his jeans. "Are you sorry?"

"Certainly not." She sat up on the desk, pulling her skirt down. "This is obviously the best way to use a desk."

"You ought to know," he said. "After all, you're an M.B.A."

She slipped off the desk and reached up to touch his cheek. "Let's go home now. To my bed."

"No."

She was startled. "Why not? Are you still angry because I didn't tell you the whole truth and nothing but?"

"Not exactly."

"I'm sorry about that, Mick. But I wanted Lil to be able to tell you herself."

He looked up sharply, noting the small quiver in her lips. "What else, Sarah?"

"And I didn't want to dump my problems with my job onto you," she admitted. "You have enough to worry about without—"

"Let me decide that. Okay, Sarah. You don't have to protect Lil. And you sure as hell don't have to protect me." He tenderly pushed a sleek wing of brown hair away from her face. "When are you going to figure out that you can't take care of everybody?"

"I don't take care of everybody."

"That's a pretty strange comment from somebody who has seven houseguests. Eight, if you include me."

"The students are leaving at the end of next week."

"And what if they can't? What if they cry on your shoulder about how they can't afford to go anywhere else?"

She shrugged. "I'll probably let them stay."

"That's why I can't go back to your house with you," he said. "Helping people is a good thing. But people take advantage of you, and you let them do it. I don't want to be one of those people."

"Why? Because Mick Pennotti works alone? Because you don't think you need anybody?" She frowned. "Can we turn off the lights in here? It's too bright."

He went to fetch a lamp from the store merchandise, and Sarah used the time to fasten her blouse and find her panties. This was crazy! She'd made love on a desktop when there was a perfectly good bed at home.

Unfortunately, her house was less private than Union Station. She'd surrounded herself with family and friends of family. Were they taking advantage of her?

Sarah recalled the few months when she'd had her house to herself. And the period before that when she lived alone in an apartment. She'd enjoyed being able to control her living space and impose order on her surroundings, but had hated being alone. Every creak in the floor had sounded like an intruder. When she'd come home from work, it had always seemed dank and cold. And lonely. Terribly lonely.

Mick set a fringed lamp in the corner and plugged it in. When he turned off the overhead fixture, the office was bathed in the amber glow of lamplight.

"Is that better?" he asked.

"Very nice." She sat in the chair behind his desk and propped her bare feet on the desktop. "Mick, I want you to come home with me. You're the only one I really want to be there."

"It won't work. You can't throw all those people out. They need your hospitality."

He was partially right. They needed her. But if Sarah was completely honest with herself, she had to accept the fact that she needed them, too. She needed people to love, to give her love to. Sarah didn't like to be alone. "I need to have people around."

"Maybe you only need one person." He lightly tasted her lips. "Maybe you only need me."

That was a lovely thought. Simple. One man—one special man—would make the perfect antidote for loneliness.

He came around the desk and sat beside her feet. When he traced a line down each sole, she shivered and said, "But we definitely need a bed."

He eyed the surface of the desk. "Do we?"

"Not always," she conceded. "But I like the modern amenities. Things like running water and a change of clothes. And food. Plus, I have to go work in the morning."

He moved his hand from her foot. His expression was serious. "What's going to happen there, Sarah?"

"Well, I'm going to spend this week putting my files in order. If I'm fired on Friday, I want the transition to another administrator to be smooth."

"Is there anything I can do to help you? I could sign a statement, promising not to sue the Werner Foundation. Or I could threaten to sue if you're fired."

She thought of Whelan and his desire to fund Mick's project. Sarah was certain that Whelan wouldn't be satisfied with an apology. Nor would he be bothered by Mick's threats. "The only thing that might make a difference would be if you filed a brand-new loan app with another administrative officer. But that's ridiculous." She hated the idea that Whelan might somehow get what he wanted. "Forget I said it."

"Will you be able to find another job?"

With a bravado she didn't truly feel, Sarah snapped her fingers and said, "In a minute. I'm good at what I do."

His hand caressed her ankle, then her calf. "You can say that again."

But words were no longer necessary. She caught his hand and tugged him toward her. Once again, they kissed.

15

ON MONDAY AFTERNOON at five o'clock, Mick waited for Sarah at her house.

Jenny had invited him to dinner, and—since he happened to be there anyway—she'd asked him to go through the attic and help her evaluate the remaining clutter for possible resale at next Saturday's flea market. He'd tried to tell her there would be no flea market—the warehouse was gone.

"Then we'll only have outdoor booths," she had replied.

"It's not safe, Jenny. I was at the site today and tried to clean up, but it's hopeless."

"Well, of course. You can't do it all by yourself." Her enthusiasm was overbearing. "Tomorrow morning, you will have Charlie and his friend in the basement, Tim. And the two student scientists. I'll drive them to the site myself. Come on, Mick. It'll be fun. Saturday can be a *real* fire sale."

"It's too much work. Even for four men."

"If you won't do it for yourself, do it for me. Please, Mick. You saved my son's life. I want to do something for you."

"It's not necessary. I didn't—"

"Then do it for Sarah," she had urged. "I'm sure she'd love to see all these houseguests put to good use."

"All right," he'd conceded. "Tomorrow morning, bring your crew and I'll put them to work."

Jenny had left him in the attic with a pile of things to evaluate and a radio that was tuned to an "oldies" station. Most of the stockpile in the attic was junk. But some was sellable.

It was hot up there. Mick peeled off his shirt and sorted through a stack of old magazines. Maybe he could keep the flea market going on a limited basis. It was a money-maker, and he could use some ready cash. But he doubted that anyone less avid than Jenny would show up to buy or to sell.

He heard light footsteps on the attic stairs. "Sarah?"

Her head, her shoulders, and finally the rest of her appeared. "What are you doing in my attic?"

"Your sister wanted me to take a look at her resale stuff."

"She's unstoppable, isn't she?" Sarah nodded toward the radio. The song that was playing was "Leader of the Pack." "That reminds me of you. It's a Harley song."

He scoffed. "Only for people who don't ride Harleys."

"Maybe that's why it works for me."

She stepped into his embrace. "You're half-naked."

"And you're not. Should we do something about that?"

"I think so."

The song on the radio changed. Vamping to the beat of "California Girls," Sarah slipped her suit jacket off her shoulders. She swirled around, tossing him a sultry backward glance. Then, swinging her hips, she kicked off both shoes, peeled off the jacket and flung it across an old steamer trunk. Still dancing, she started on the buttons of her blouse.

"Very nice." He applauded.

"Yeah," came an echo from the staircase.

"Auntie Sarah, I didn't know you could dance."

Jamie and Joey bounced up the last two steps, and Sarah thanked her lucky stars that she hadn't been cavorting in the nude. She grabbed Jamie's hands and drew him into it. "Of course, I can dance," she said. "And so can you."

"Not me." Joey glared at his younger brother. "That's girl stuff. Guys don't have to dance."

"Wrong," said Mick. "Guys like to dance with girls."

"Oh yeah? Well, I don't see you doing it."

Mick tapped Jamie on the shoulder. "May I cut in?"

Since the beat was rock and roll, Mick grasped her fingertips lightly. They spun toward each other, nearly embracing, then twirled apart.

Despite the presence of the two little boys, Sarah felt the excitement of being near Mick as she danced close to him. It was all too soon when he swung her into his arms for a final dip.

"Ta-da!" Mick said.

"That was sick," Joey commented.

"I like it," his little brother piped up.

Before the two boys could launch into a full-fledged battle on the merits of dancing with girls, their mother's voice resounded in the stairwell. "Time for dinner!"

The children dashed down the stairs.

"Privacy." Mick rolled his eyes. "For two minutes it's just you and me, Sarah. And where were we?"

"I believe I was stripping."

"Well, I guess the moment has passed. Dinner's ready."

She gathered up her jacket and slid her feet back into her shoes. It was difficult to sustain a sexual excitement when she visualized the nephews, sister, brother and assorted guests with their ear at the attic door.

Mick sensed her reluctance. "Before we go down there, tell me about your day. Anything new at work?"

"It was quiet. Very quiet." Ray Innis hadn't said more than ten words to her. And neither Whelan nor Frank Chapperal had been around. "I got a lot done. How about you?"

"I ran a tally of the claims you wrote down from people who lost merchandise at the flea market. It's a bundle."

"Don't worry about it. Nobody will expect compensation until the insurance company pays you. Did you get all your claim forms filled?"

"Yeah. My insurance agent, Larry Atwater, is supposed to call me here within the hour."

"Is there a problem?"

"Is the sky blue? Of course, there's a problem. Everything in my life is a problem." He took her hand and pulled her against him. "Except for you. I can't stop thinking about you."

"Funny thing." She reached behind his shoulder and tugged on his ponytail. "I feel the same."

This time, Charlie's voice bellowed up the stairs. "Dinner time. Come on, Sarah and Mick, before it gets cold!"

They sighed. Food seemed unimportant. All the other complications in life were minuscule compared to what they felt for each other.

Descending the stairs to the main floor of the house was like entering the eye of a tornado. Joey and Jamie streaked past carrying napkins. Charlie and Tim brought dishes from the kitchen. The two students were already seated at the table. Though Sarah bordered on saying something rude about the mob, she restrained herself.

Many of these people would leave soon. With luck, she'd still have a grip on her sanity when they were gone.

When the entire horde had settled at the large dining-room table, every seat was occupied. Sarah counted nine people.

Jenny tapped her water glass with a spoon and waited for silence. "Before we eat, I'd like to offer a brief prayer." She lowered her eyes. "Thank you, God, for sending Mick to help us."

Sarah gazed around the table at the bowed heads. Though her home was chaotic and these people might be taking advantage of her, she felt warm. This was her family. Moments like these were supposed to make life worth living. Yet, she knew it would all be empty without Mick. His presence beside her made her feel as if she really had a family. Beneath the table, she slipped her hand into his.

Jenny continued, "Mick's courage when he rescued my little boy was a blessing. Though I've promised him I won't say anything more about his heroism, I will be eternally grateful in my heart. Amen."

Sarah watched as eight other sets of hands grabbed for first helpings. She listened as the conversation rose to a ruckus. When the telephone rang, she could barely hear it.

Jenny answered, then turned to Mick. "It's for you. The man says his name is Larry Atwater."

"My insurance agent."

Sarah advised, "Take your call on the kitchen extension. I'll hang up in here."

Mick hurried through the swing doors. Since Jenny had been cooking up a storm, it was hot in the kitchen. But that wasn't the only reason he'd begun to sweat. "Okay, Larry. What's the story?"

"Bad news. The parent company won't reimburse you for the break-in at Penny Wise until their accountants have checked your ledgers against your claim of cash in the safe."

"Seems fair," Mick said. "I'll get copies of my books to you by tomorrow morning. What about the flea market? That was a fire—straightforward and simple. How much do I get?"

"You'll get the full damages to the building and to your trailer, but there's going to be a wait."

The tension in Mick's shoulders centered at the base of his neck. "What about the claims from flea-market merchants? Is the company going to honor those?"

"I'm sorry, Mick. We'll take care of personal-injury claims, but as for their merchandise? Well, I'm afraid there's nothing in your policies to cover that."

"Okay. I'll find a way to handle that myself. But I don't understand why there's a wait on my payout."

"The company plans to investigate the fire as a possible arson."

"Not a chance of that," Mick told his agent. "It was an accident. There were witnesses."

"I'm sorry, but you can appreciate our position. You've had two substantial claims in less than a week. The coincidence can't be ignored. Is there any possibility that someone is trying to hurt you, Mick?"

"No." The two disasters had been simple bad luck. Mick rubbed his forehead, feeling a headache coming on. "No chance that these things were sabotage."

"Then I don't know what to tell you, except that you'll have to wait until our investigators are through."

"Why? I've paid my premiums. Why can't I get what I paid for? I need the money now, Larry."

"Maybe that's the problem. How **ba**dly do you need cash?"

Mick had been in business long enough to fully comprehend this innuendo. The problem—the real problem—wasn't any kind of figuring of ledgers or reports from investigators. The problem was that he operated businesses that were on the fringe of respectability, and insurance companies didn't like to pay off to renegades. They were suspicious of him. They figured he was trying to pull something, trying to defraud the company.

"Let me see if I understand," Mick said. "Suppose I was a lawyer whose safe in his office was robbed. Then you'd pay me. Right? If I was a nice lady whose doll shop burned to the ground, you'd pay. Right?"

"I can't answer that."

"But we both know the answer, don't we?" Mick repressed his disgust. Right now, it was important for him to be coherent. "Level with me, Larry. What do I need to do?"

"It'd help a lot if you could prove that the theft at Penny Wise was, in fact, a theft. An eyewitness would be good."

"I've got a witness." A sixteen-year-old with wild hair and a tattoo. Lil wasn't exactly an insurance company's idea of reliable. Mick's headaches intensified. "What else, Larry?"

"That's about all. I'm sorry, Mick. This could take anywhere from two weeks to a couple of months."

Mick hung up the telephone and looked for something he could break, some way to let off the pressure that was building inside him. He placed both palms on the cool surface of the refrigerator and rested his forehead between them.

He felt Sarah's approach before she actually spoke.

"I know it doesn't seem likely," she said, "but this will all work out. The insurance company is required to pay."

"In their own sweet time," he said.

"Why are you in such a hurry?"

"It's not for me." He turned around to face her. "I can get by on the profits from the estate sale and the money I've got saved for the warehouse project. But I'm worried about the flea-market vendors. I want to pay back every cent to them."

"They can wait." Sarah knew the merchants had suffered a setback, but their losses weren't devastating. Since the fire had come at the end of the day, most of them had begun to clear out their booths, anyway. Most claims were under two hundred dollars—small amounts considered individually.

"I want to pay them," he persisted. "I don't want to be like that guy who screwed my family. He made promises and didn't come through."

"It's not the same thing," she argued. Taking both his hands in her own, she spoke the very words he'd recited to her: "You can't take care of everybody else, Mick. People have to handle their own problems."

"It doesn't feel right."

"But it *is* right. Trust me. I'm an M.B.A., you know."

Her touch on his arm was soothing, but Mick's mind was racing faster than his Harley on an open stretch of road. "Is that Werner Foundation money still available?"

"Probably." She frowned. "But you'd still have to use your land as collateral."

And it would still be a loan. On the other hand, if he took the Werner Foundation loan, he could repay the flea-market merchants, plus, he could start immediate construction on his warehouses. The idea of building felt good. All the people in his family were builders. Some of his earliest memories included the laying of foundations and putting up frameworks. Heavy work. Satisfying work.

Expensive work. "I might just take that loan."

Before Sarah could comment pro or con, Jenny pushed open the door to the kitchen. "Come back to the table, both of you. This dinner is in your honor, Mick."

"I'm going to have to beg off," he said. "I have a killer headache. Guess I'd better take off. Sorry."

"No problem." Jenny's hospitality was undeterred. "But if you need to rest, why don't you stay here tonight?"

"To relax?" Sarah questioned. "In this house? A buffalo stampede would be more conducive to rest."

"Fine," Jenny snapped at her sister. "Then you pack Mick a doggie bag. Wherever he sleeps, he needs to eat."

When she turned on her heel and went back to the dining room, Sarah looked up at Mick. "Do you really have a headache?"

"You know me. I don't lie." He smiled. "But I expect it'll be gone in an hour. Meet me at Penny Wise."

He kissed her quickly. Then he left.

She waited in the kitchen until she heard the roar of his Harley in the driveway before returning to the table. The meal passed at a tortoise's pace. Sarah felt fidgety, anxious for an hour to pass.

Mick had raised an interesting question. If he took the loan, would she be off the hook? She expected that Whelan—who was probably pushing for her dismissal—would be appeased. And yet, the fact of her behavior hadn't changed.

At last, the hour was up. Sarah crept out the back door and drove to Penny Wise. From habit, she went to the rear entry and knocked. "Mick?"

"It's open," he called out.

It was almost dark inside the store. Sarah closed the door and locked it behind her. "What's going on, Mick?"

"Walk carefully," he advised.

When she stopped around the partition at the rear and into the shop, Sarah saw dozens of votive candles. Their flickering illumination made a path to a gleaming brass bed where Mick awaited her. His lower body was covered with a handmade quilt.

"How romantic," Sarah said. Then her practical side kicked in. "This isn't a fire hazard, is it?"

"No. The candles are all in containers. A while back, I bought the overstock at an archdiocese garage sale."

Silently she lay down beside him. When their lips met, Sarah tasted the familiar fulfillment. She had begun to understand the nuances of their lovemaking. Yet, every time she touched him, the thrill was brand-new.

She undressed quickly, and when their naked bodies met, Sarah closed her eyes in delight and pleasure. He felt so good against her and his caresses touched her in exactly the right places.

"Sarah," he said softly. "I miss the unicorn."

When she gazed at his features, alight with the glow from candles, she thought he was the most handsome man she'd ever known. "It was only meant to be temporary."

"Guess so," he said. "I hoped it would be there forever."

Forever. Did she dare to think of "forever" with Mick? They hadn't spoken of commitment. For now, making love was enough.

As her taut nipples grazed the hair on his chest, she felt an electric response. When his lips tasted hers, she arched tightly, hungrily against him. At last his penis slid into her ready slick warmth and his thrusts drove her in a throbbing, bucking rhythm. Harder and harder....

Then ecstasy enveloped her.

Later, as she lay beside him, Sarah imagined that this was their home. Hers and Mick's, alone. Just the two of them. Every night they would share dinner and conversation about work. Then they would go to bed together, make love until dawn.

She cuddled close to him, reveling in the feel of his naked flesh against hers.

EVERY NIGHT for the next three nights at Penny Wise, Mick surprised her with flowers and incense and soft music.

On Thursday night, she planned to leave early. Friday was the board meeting at the Werner Foundation. On Friday morning, she would learn if she was going to be fired.

When Sarah slipped from the bed and began dressing, Mick asked, "Your board meeting is tomorrow. Aren't you scared?"

"Not really. I'm anxious for it to be over."

"I know what you mean."

He seemed preoccupied. But why shouldn't he be? Despite Lil's confession to the police, there had been no definite word on his payment from the insurance company. And he had put off contacting the flea-market merchants regarding compensation. Also, though the site was barely cleaned up from the fire, Jenny had plastered the town with fliers announcing the reopening of Mick's flea market.

"I'm sorry about Jenny's interference," she said.

"It's okay. She's trying to help." His laugh was bitter. "As if there will be any customers at a burned-down market. I expect that the only people who are going to show will be the ones who really need money from me."

"Mick, you've got to let those people take care of their own loss. You have enough to worry about."

"But I let them down. I promised there would always be a flea market. And even after I built the warehouses, I would have maintained the marketplace." He frowned. "I've betrayed all those good people who trusted me."

"The fire wasn't your fault, Mick."

"I know. But it feels like it was."

His hair fell around his shoulders. His lips were set in a grimace, and Sarah longed to make it better, to see him smile. "I love you," she said.

The words just slipped out. She hadn't meant to say them, but she couldn't hold back any longer.

"What did you say?" he asked.

"Nothing." She'd spoken too soon. There were too many other things to consider.

He gently reached out and took her hand. "And I love you, too."

She gave a small cry and embraced him. Never had she expected to hear those words from him. She'd never dreamed she'd hear him say that he loved her.

That night, their lovemaking reached new heights, ran the gamut from slow and leisurely to a fierce expression of need. Tonight was special. They were in love. They were lovers. And truly, they shared a grand passion.

Sarah wished that tomorrow would never come.

16

SARAH AWOKE TO FACE another Friday. It had been a Friday, only a week ago, when she'd made love to Mick for the first time. Now her life had changed—irreparably and wonderfully.

She hoped the board meeting would also be a change for the good. But, frankly, she doubted it. She rolled onto her side in the bed and looked at Mick—he looked so appealing. But Sarah didn't dare kiss him. One kiss would lead to another, and the light was already breaking through the storefront windows.

"They're going to fire me," she muttered, forcing herself out of their warm bed. "I can feel it."

"Don't be so sure."

"A couple of weeks ago, I would have thought being fired was the end of my life. Now it doesn't seem so awful."

"What happens if you are?"

"It's not like the army where they rip off your stripes. Maybe they'll take away my business cards and run them through the shredder."

Mick chuckled. "You don't seem too upset."

"I'm not." She leaned across the bed and kissed him. She sighed. "Thanks to you, Mr. Michael Pennotti, I'm not devastated at the thought of losing my job."

Leaving Mick was always hard, but today seemed more difficult than usual. It took all her willpower to depart from Penny Wise and return home to change into her most severe business suit. And then she waited. The board meeting was scheduled for ten o'clock, and Sarah had calculated her arrival so that she'd have just enough time to take the elevator to the upper floor of the Werner Foundation offices.

Outside the boardroom, she greeted the secretary stationed at the reception desk. Then, pushing the doors wide, Sarah entered the conference room.

Frank Chapperal rose and directed her to a seat. He offered a friendly greeting, and Sarah responded. She had been to dozens of board meetings and knew most of these men and women on a first-name basis. When she spied Donald Whelan with Ray Innis at his side, she even managed to smile at them.

The chairman spoke: "Shall we begin?"

He ran through the proposed agenda and concluded with, "I suggest we start with a discussion of the Pennotti loan."

Sarah heard the door behind her open. She heard the shrill tones of the secretary, protesting that the meeting was closed. Then she saw Mick, striding to the head of the table.

"I'll take your loan," he said. He pitched an application onto the gleaming tabletop. "Here's a new app. Filled out and signed by me. I'll use my land as collateral."

"No!" Sarah rose to her feet. "You don't have to do this."

"I want to." He smiled at her. The most wonderful smile in the world. "I want to start building my warehouses."

"Thank you," said Frank Chapperal, quickly. "And I believe this concludes our discussion of Mr. Pennotti's loan. I suggest that we assign Ray Innis to processing this loan. Next item?"

Sarah couldn't believe it. She was going to get off the hook. Her affair with Mick wouldn't even be mentioned.

But Mick hadn't left the boardroom. His gaze shot across the table and stuck on Don Whelan. Mick's smile became a snarl. "You!" he exclaimed.

Outrage surged through Mick's body like a physical force, as if a knife had been thrust into the center of his back. Don Whelan had been in construction, had made his money during the housing boom. Don Whelan was the snake who had destroyed Mick's family with his false promises.

He stared at Sarah. He'd wanted to take the loan partly for her. He'd wanted to build something with her. But she had deceived him. From the beginning, she must have known about Whelan. How could she have done this to him?

Whelan was talking. To Mick, his voice sounded oily. "You probably won't believe this, Mick. But I've wanted to make amends to your family—for years."

"You're right. I don't believe it."

"When I saw your loan application, I thought this might be a way I could help."

"Help yourself to my land. Right?"

"No, Mick. That's not it. I believe your warehouse project had merit. I made a mistake with your father. Let me apologize through you."

"Save your apology for someone who wants to hear it."

Mick struggled to control the pain and anger that raged inside him, blanking out hope. Sarah had been the only woman—practically the only person—he'd trusted in years. And he'd been wrong. "Save your lies for Sarah."

"Oh, my God," she whispered.

Her voice sounded tiny and afraid. But Mick had no desire to comfort her.

Painfully, she asked, "Whelan was the person who caused your father to go out of business, wasn't he?"

"You know he was. Don Whelan came out of it a rich man. And my father lost everything."

His fists clenched and he cursed himself for ever trusting Sarah. He'd been a jerk to believe she actually cared for him. She was just doing her job—the job that she loved—working for that bastard Whelan.

Her face swam into his view, and he heard her denial, "I didn't know, Mick."

"Stop lying. How could you not know?"

"Please believe me!"

Mick wrenched his gaze away from her. Her affection had been poison. And her love? The love she'd supposedly felt for him? A lie. He pivoted on his heel and left the boardroom.

"Wait!" she called after him. "Wait, Mick."

But he was gone.

"Sarah," Frank Chapperal interjected. "Would you please be seated."

She turned to Whelan. "Why didn't you tell me?"

"About the connection between Mick's father and myself? I didn't believe it was necessary. Besides, it's all turned out for the best. Mick will have his loan. He'll be able to start building. Hopefully, he'll make a tidy profit."

"And that's the only thing that's important, right? Profit and loss. Give and take."

"In business, that's all there is."

"So, if Mick succeeds, your conscience will be appeased for destroying his family. What about the emotional toll? What about the pain?"

"There's always a cost to doing business."

Whelan leaned back in his chair. She saw that again, he was playing with the little rubber ball, squeezing it, curling and uncurling his fingers around it. Beside him, Ray Innis maintained a proper blank expression. And the other faces, ranged around the table, showed a cool unconcern. If there were any emotion, it was embarrassment over her outburst.

"If doing business means a license to hurt people, I want no part of it." Sarah gathered her papers and stuffed them into her briefcase. "I thought the Werner Foundation was different, that we based our decisions on more than dollars and cents. But I was wrong. Ladies and gentlemen of the board, I resign."

Her frustrated anger drove her from the room, onto the elevator and down to the basement parking. It wasn't until she was behind the wheel of her car that Sarah fully exhaled the breath she'd been holding and collapsed against the seat.

What had she done?

Quit her job. A job that had paid the bills and given her a measure of satisfaction. Worse than that, she'd unknowingly betrayed Mick. He'd never forgive her. He'd never trust her. Even if he still loved her, there could never be a commitment between them. Trust was essential. And Mick's fragile trust in her had been shattered.

"It's not my fault," she murmured to herself. But it was. She should have done more research on Whelan when he started showing such intense interest in Mick's project. Surely his connection with Mick's father was a matter of public record. She should have known. Someone like Ray Innis would have researched thoroughly. But Sarah had been stupid enough to trust that a board member of the Werner Foundation wasn't really a slime. And there hadn't been enough time. There was her other workload. And there were all these people staying with her, and the break-in and the fire and the theft.

Poor excuses when she considered the result. She should have known better. If she'd performed her job at the peak of her ability, she wouldn't have lost the one man who was most important in her life.

She had to find him. She had to at least try to convince him that she hadn't known about Whelan's connection with his family.

Her fingers moved mechanically, twisting the car key in the ignition. First, she went to Penny Wise. Mick wasn't there.

She had to find him, just had to. She went to the deli next door. They hadn't seen Mick. At the tattoo parlor beside the deli, Sarah stayed for an hour. If she couldn't have Mick, she would give herself something to remember him by.

Then she drove the long miles out to the warehouse site. Her heart wouldn't stop hammering. Breathing was so difficult that she pulled over to the shoulder of the highway and waited for her intense panic to subside.

Oh, why did it have to be Whelan? She remembered Mick's hatred when he talked about the devastation of his family, the destruction of his father's self-respect, the uprooting of the Pennotti business. Because of lies. Because of Whelan.

She knew that Mick wasn't rational when it came to Whelan's betrayal. Therefore it was up to Sarah to be calm and sane. She touched her fingers to her pulse, willing herself to breathe evenly.

But when she found Mick, what would she say?

Unfortunately there was no defense. All she could offer was her word. She'd been inefficient. She hadn't behaved in her usual professional manner in checking out Whelan.

And if he wouldn't accept her word?

It was better to find out now. If he couldn't trust her completely, they didn't have much chance for a future.

Clearheaded at last, she drove to the site of the former flea market.

Before she was very far along the winding turnoff, she could see activity at the site. Charlie and Tim and the students were busily clearing the rubble and setting up barriers to keep people from stepping into the fire-blackened ruins.

Sarah didn't particularly want to talk to her brother, but she needed to know if Mick had been here. She parked and went to him. "Have you seen Mick?"

"Not today." He gestured proudly at their cleanup efforts. "What do you think?"

"Looks good."

"Something's wrong, Sarah. You can tell me. I'm almost a psychologist."

"A problem between me and Mick." She looked up at her tall brother. "I really don't want to talk about it."

"Okay." He nodded. "But let me tell you something that will cheer you up. Tim's going to be moving out tonight. He got back together with his girlfriend."

"Swell."

"There's more. I've got an apartment of my own. In two weeks, I'll be out of your basement." He hugged her. "You've been great to put up with me, but I can't be an irresponsible student forever. When Jamie was almost killed in that fire, I decided it was time to get myself some priorities. To do something with my life."

Sarah managed a smile. "What would Freud say about that?"

"He'd say: 'Welcome to the adult world. It's about time.'"

Sarah swallowed the lump in her throat. What would Freud say about the surprising sadness she felt when she thought of Charlie leaving the nest? The students would be gone after the weekend. In a few months, Jenny and her nephews would also be leaving. Sarah would have her house back—two floors, an attic and a basement. She'd have her privacy. And it would seem as empty as an Arctic wasteland.

The catch in her voice was genuine when she said, "I'll miss you, baby brother."

"You'll love it," he predicted. "You and Mick can rattle around in that big old house. Just the two of you."

She nodded. It could have been lovely.

Pulling herself together so that Charlie wouldn't worry, Sarah left the warehouse site and drove the long miles back toward town.

The mountains that ranged before her were beautiful today, their grandeur unobscured by pollution. Unmelted snowcaps glistened whitely in the sun. Perhaps Mick was there. He might have jumped on his Harley and driven west. Was he, at this very moment, shouting his frustration into the wind? The mountains could be a powerful consolation. They were so majestic—and remote.

Soon, Sarah feared, she would be alone. Like Clara, the tragic opera singer who had waited too long for passion—

Clara's. Perhaps Mick had gone there—the first place where they'd made love.

It was late afternoon when Sarah pulled up in front of the narrow two-story house. A realtor's sign was planted in the front yard. There was an emptiness about the place. A sense of vacancy. No one lived here anymore.

Though she didn't see Mick's Harley, Sarah parked and went to the porch to peer through the windows. Inside, the floors were bare. All of Clara's things had been removed, and every trace of her was gone.

Cherished memories. Sarah sat on the porch swing. She could see the flowers blooming. Butterflies flitted in the fading light. It might be wise to forget about Mick. To hold the memories and move on with her life.

But she wanted Mick and his love. She wanted to build a life with him. He had to understand. Once she'd explained, he would see that she hadn't betrayed him.

And still she sat there, swinging on the porch, watching as the dusk settled. Lightly she massaged the tender skin above her breast and was overwhelmed by feelings of desolation.

She glanced at her wristwatch. Seven o'clock. Penny Wise would be closed. Sooner or later, she figured, Mick would return there to sleep. She would find him. She would explain. Maybe he'd already forgiven her.

With a heavy heart, she left and went to Penny Wise. Mick had to be there.

Parked at the rear, she saw his Harley. Her sense of relief was tinged with fear. At least she would be able to face him. At least they could try to work this out. Flinging open the door to her car, she went to the rear entrance. The door was ajar.

From inside the store, she heard a crash. Sarah started. What was going on in there?

Another crash. Was Mick in trouble?

When she pushed it, the door swung wide. Mick stood some distance from her, not seeing her. His hair hung loose and his face and T-shirt were streaked with dirt. He looked like a wild man. His powerful arms tightened as he picked up a small vase, stared at it, then hurled it to the floor where it exploded into a million shards. He kicked at a rocking chair, overturning it. The brass bed where they had slept was already torn apart. The mattress askew.

The force of his rage overwhelmed her, and Sarah knew that he would never forgive her. Would never forget.

His hand reached for a porcelain doll. From where she stood, Sarah couldn't tell if it was the exact doll she'd admired when she first came into the store. She saw his fury in the way he gripped the doll, ruthlessly crushing its velvet skirts.

She covered her mouth with her hand, holding back an anguished cry. Oh, God, did he hate her that much?

17

IN HORROR, SARAH FLED from the store. Leaving the rear door, she ran to her car. She had to go home, to the place where she could be safe.

Through his dank despair, Mick had sensed her presence. "Sarah," he whispered.

Whirling around, he faced the rear of the store, holding the doll that would always remind him of Sarah . . . Sarah . . . Sarah. . . . The door was open. But there was no one there.

He heard a car start. "Sarah!"

He strode through the mess on the floor—*his* mess. Bits of glass ground to dust beneath his heavy motorcycle boots. From the rear of the shop, he saw taillights at the end of the alley.

His shoulders slumped. Returning inside, he gently placed the doll on a spindle-legged table. His fingers smoothed its gown, gave a lingering caress to the painted rosebud mouth. He braced his arms on the table, lowered his head and breathed heavily.

She'd lied to him. She'd told Mick that *somebody* had been pushing her to make the loan, but she had concealed Whelan's identity. Like Lil, he thought. Sarah hadn't actually lied, but she hadn't told him everything. Her first instinct had been to protect the Werner Foundation.

He ought to hate her. Couldn't trust the damn woman. But why couldn't he erase her image from his mind?

"Damn it." He grabbed a ceramic lamp and held it over his head, ready to smash the thing to bits.

But what was the point? There'd been a time in his life—not so long ago—when he would have demolished this place, would have ridden his bike through the store and out the front window. But he was older now. More mature.

He wanted to build, not tear things apart.

He would take a loan to pay his bills—if that meant he could build a future with Sarah.

SARAH SLEPT FITFULLY and woke before everyone else in her house. Not wanting to face her family, she dressed quickly and departed. In the predawn stillness, she drove the familiar route to the flea-market site.

At the end of the winding road that exited from the highway, she drove past the only structure that had been left standing after the fire—the ticket-taking booth. The flea-market area was filled with signs of Charlie's repairs and handiwork. She pulled up beside the Park Here sign and sat huddled in her car.

When she saw a single headlight bobbing along the road, her heart wrenched in her chest. It had to be Mick's Harley. Sarah twisted her cold fingers together. In minutes, she would face him. Her future would be decided.

The Harley pulled up beside her car. In the thin light, she saw him yank off his helmet. His hair was pulled back neatly in a ponytail.

Now or never. She opened her car door. "Mick. We have to talk."

"No kidding, Sarah." He dismounted the Harley and came toward her. "I'll go first."

She nodded.

"When I saw Whelan sitting in that boardroom with his expensive suit and his gold cuff-links, I lost it. I hate that son of a bitch. And that won't change. Not ever."

"I understand. Mick, if I had ever thought, even for a minute, that—"

"Hold it." He raised his hand. "I'm still talking."

He stared at her. Her smooth brown hair, her ivory complexion—God, she was beautiful. And as fragile as that porcelain doll. How could those lips have spoken lies?

"But there are some changes," he said. "I'm going to take that loan from the Werner Foundation."

He scanned the flat plains beyond the warehouse. "It's time. It's time for me to take my dreams and make them work." He looked back at her. "And I'll make it work between us, too."

"Do you love me, Mick?"

He sighed. "God help me. I do."

"But you don't trust me."

"No."

"Then it won't work. No matter how much you try to forgive me, there'll be doubt. A seed of disappointment. You'll keep secrets. You'll never be able to look at me without regret."

He straightened his shoulders. "Okay, Sarah. If you want to forget this whole thing, that's fine with me. Fine."

"No. I don't *want* to." Even in the pale light, he could see her eyes blaze. "But I won't spend my life wondering if you hate me."

"You should have thought of that before you lied to me."

"I didn't lie. When Whelan started taking such an interest in your project, I should have been suspicious enough to do some research on him. But I didn't. I didn't know there was a connection between your family and Don Whelan."

"Even if that's true, why didn't you tell me about this guy who was hot for my project? Why didn't you mention his name? Face it, Sarah. You were protecting your job, and I came second."

"My job?" She laughed. "I don't have a job, Mick. I resigned."

"You quit your job for me?"

"Not for you. For myself. All these years, I'd thought I was working for a business with a heart. I thought the foundation considered more than profit and loss to make their decisions. I was wrong. If someone like Whelan can be on the board, I want no part of the Werner Foundation."

He felt as if a weight had been lifted from his shoulders. "You didn't know."

"I should have known, should have researched Whelan. But it never occurred to me that a member of the board could be dishonorable. Not even when he tried to blackmail me."

"Blackmail?"

"That was the phone call I received last Sunday morning. Whelan told me to back off on your loan or he would make sure that I was fired for inappropriate behavior."

"You should have told me."

"Maybe so. But I managed to deal with it myself by calling in Frank Chapperal. Then he told me about Lil, and I thought everything was under control."

Mick studied Sarah. She looked weary. Dark shadows beneath her eyes attested to a sleepless night. Yet her strength, her honesty was clearly evident. "I always hoped I could believe in you, Sarah."

"You can."

"I know." Turning on his heel, Mick went to his motorcycle. From the rear compartment, he removed an object wrapped in a towel. "Last night, I wanted to destroy everything. To tear my sorry life to shreds. I was at Penny Wise, smashing all that cheap glass junk. Then I saw this."

He handed her the package.

When Sarah unwrapped the towel, she saw the porcelain doll. Her doll. It was the first object that had touched her when she entered Mick's world and it was the last thing she'd seen him with last night. He hadn't broken it.

Carefully she placed the doll on the hood of her car, and then stepped into his embrace. His arms, clad in his leather riding jacket, were cold and hard, but soon his body warmed her. The contrast of his heat against the chill and the fire of his kiss sent shivers racing up and down her spine. Thank God, they'd made up. She couldn't imagine not ever feeling his arms around her again.

His voice was husky. "Let's get out of here."

"We can't leave," she said. "The flea-market merchants are going to be arriving any minute."

"Get real, Sarah. Nobody's coming, except for your crazy sister. There is no more flea market." His gaze was caught by a bit of bright crepe paper fluttering in the wind. "It was a nice thought, but dumb."

Despite the cleanup, the place was a ruin. The charred remains of the warehouse were roped off. His trailer—standing amid the burned-out trunks of trees—was a wreck.

"I don't know why I bothered to come out here."

"Because you have an obligation," Sarah informed him. "You didn't contact people and tell them not to show up. You didn't close down."

"I should have. This part of my life is over—except for paying everybody back on their losses."

"Maybe not, Mick."

Her hopefulness was endearing, but futile. Sure, it would have been nice to keep the flea market going. The extra cash would have come in handy. But he didn't believe it would happen. Besides, the more important event had already occurred. He had rediscovered his trust in Sarah. And that was all that mattered.

Lightly he kissed her forehead. "One miracle per sunrise is all anybody can expect."

"Brace yourself for another."

She pointed to the road where the headlights of two cars were beaming.

"Jenny and Charlie," Mick said dismissively.

"And somebody else." The headlights from a third vehicle followed the road to the warehouse. "They'll come," Sarah assured him. "Nobody wants to let you down, Mick. These people care about you."

"Three cars," he said. "Maybe two or three more. Some rats don't know when to desert a sinking ship."

Yet, he greeted Jenny and Charlie and the other vendor like old and dear friends. For so many years, he'd been alone. Didn't trust anyone but himself. Even these few people gave him reason to believe in other people.

Another car headed down the road. And another.

Then came a caravan of farmers' trucks.

It seemed that the sun was rising on a brand-new venture.

"I knew there'd be merchants here," Jenny continued. "In fact, I telephoned a few of them to remind them we'd be open."

"What?" Mick demanded. "You did what?"

"Well, I couldn't let the flea market die. This is a good way for me to make money. Plus, there was that notebook full of names and phone numbers just lying around. And I talked to the newspaper that had Sarah's picture on the front page. There was a little article yesterday. Oh, yes—and there was that television interview last night. Jamie and Joey were so cute."

"Television interview?"

"Channel Two. A two-minute news special. Headline—Denver Merchants Won't Give Up. A Real Fire Sale. Believe me, Mick, everybody's excited that you're going to stay open."

Mick laughed. "You're a pushy broad, Jenny."

"And aren't you glad that I am?"

Nearly half of the regular flea-market merchants had arrived before eight o'clock in the morning. As Sarah watched the colorful makeshift booths being assembled on the asphalt parking lot, she admired their determination. A real fire sale. These were people who overcame the odds; people who wouldn't give up. They were survivors.

Last week, they'd lost some of their wares but escaped with their lives. They'd rested. And now, they were ready to pick up and start over again. Just as she would. She'd find a new job, start a new life.

When Mick finished helping a farmer with a load of cantaloupes, Sarah joined him. "Surprised?"

"Hell, yes." In wonderment, he gazed at the renewed flea market. Banners and tents and signs. Despite the persistent smell of smoke, the air was filled with laughter. "I can't believe this. It's like a carnival."

"I guess nobody told them they should be depressed. Or angry at you."

"They're not, are they?" He was dumbfounded, positively amazed. "Some people told me that if the insurance company wasn't paying, I could forget their claim. They just want me to open again on a regular basis."

"Maybe, just maybe, they care about you."

When the first carload of customers rolled down the road, a cheer went up from the crowd. Then came another carload. And another. By noon, the flea market was full of activity. Mick estimated that there were more customers than usual.

In fact, the day was so hectic that Sarah didn't have a moment alone with Mick until closing time. When the last car pulled out of the lot, its occupants waving and promising to be back on the following day, she collapsed into his arms. "Tomorrow? Are we going to do this tomorrow?"

"You bet! It's great, huh?"

"Sure. Keen."

"I'm going to rebuild, Sarah. Starting on Monday. With a couple of temporary structures here, and rewiring. I'll pay people back by getting the flea market up and running again." He tightened his arms around her. "Of course, I still plan to take that Werner Foundation money."

"You should contact Ray Innis."

"He already contacted me. Showed up around noon. That guy is nearly as persistent as you were."

She grinned. "He's a lot more aggressive than I ever was."

"But not as sharp. Anybody can be efficient. But you're more than that." He nuzzled her cheek. "You have the wisdom that comes from caring."

"And an M.B.A.," she added.

"Yeah, Ms. Businesswoman. But it occurs to me that you happen to be unemployed."

"I guess I am."

"I'd like to hire you. Full-time."

"And do you have an opening for an executive administrator?"

"How about business manager? Analyst. Accountant. Somebody who tells me when I've screwed up."

"Every screwup?" She grinned wryly. "A full-time job."

"That's right, smartass. And when I get started with the warehouses, I'm going to need somebody."

"I don't know." Working for Mick? She couldn't think of a better job. Or a more challenging one. When he started his warehouse distribution operations, the organizational details would be massive. She teased, "Can you pay me what I'm worth?"

"Probably not."

Sarah leaned away from him and studied his expression. "You're serious about this, aren't you?"

"Damn right. I'd like for you to be my partner."

Any doubt she might have had about Mick's trust vanished like smoke in a high wind. His offer meant the world to her, and yet she hesitated. "I'm not sure if I'd be the right person. I should think about this."

"Maybe you'd better. Because I'm looking for a lifetime commitment." He gazed into her eyes. "Are you ready for that, Sarah?"

"Something permanent?"

He nodded.

Sarah stepped away from him. She unfastened the top two buttons on her shirt and pushed the fabric aside to reveal a tiny unicorn tattoo on the skin above her breast. "Is that permanent enough for you?"

"When did you do that?"

"Yesterday. At the shop down the street from your store. I thought I was going to lose you, and I wanted a memory."

He bent one knee to the asphalt pavement. "Will you be my partner . . . and my wife?"

His wife? Had she heard him correctly?

"I love you, Sarah. I want to spend every day exactly like we've spent this one. Working together from sunrise to sunset. And every night, I want you beside me in my bed—being together, being as one."

"Every sunrise?"

"Dawn to dusk."

"I love you, too." She took his hand and with a slight tug brought him to his feet and into her arms. "I can't wait to be your wife. But can we live at my house? I mean, the bed at Penny Wise is great, but I really like my house."

He nuzzled her throat. "Is that tattoo sore?"

"A little."

"Can I kiss it and make it better?"

"Mick! We were discussing living arrangements. Can we live at my house?"

"Yes, you stubborn woman. As soon as you get rid of all the houseguests."

"Just you and me," she promised.

"Then I'd say this negotiation is over."

"Except for the traditional handshake to consummate the deal."

"If you think I'm going to be happy with just a handshake, you've got a lot to learn, partner."

Sarah had a feeling their future together would be brilliant—and a passion more grand than any she could imagine.

She knew they would trust each other enough to dream, to create new fantasies. Their love was no longer a risky proposition.

HARLEQUIN *Temptation*

Rebels & Rogues

Quinn: He was a real-life hero to everyone except himself.

THE MIGHTY QUINN
by Candace Schuler
Temptation #397, June 1992

All men are not created equal. Some are rough around the edges. Tough-minded but tenderhearted. Incredibly sexy. The tempting fulfillment of every woman's fantasy.

When it's time to fight for what they believe in, to win that special woman, our Rebels and Rogues are heroes at heart. Twelve Rebels and Rogues, one each month in 1992, only from Harlequin Temptation!

◈ Harlequin®

JANELLE TAYLOR

Valley of Fire

HARLEQUIN IS PROUD TO PRESENT *VALLEY OF FIRE* BY JANELLE TAYLOR—AUTHOR OF TWENTY-TWO BOOKS, INCLUDING SIX *NEW YORK TIMES* BESTSELLERS

VALLEY OF FIRE—the warm and passionate story of Kathy Alexander, a famous romance author, and Steven Winngate, entrepreneur and owner of the magazine that intended to expose the real Kathy "Brandy" Alexander to her fans.

Don't miss VALLEY OF FIRE, available in May.

FREE GIFT OFFER

To receive your free gift, send us the specified number of proofs-of-purchase from any specially marked Free Gift Offer Harlequin or Silhouette book with the Free Gift Certificate properly completed, plus a check or money order (do not send cash) to cover postage and handling payable to Harlequin/Silhouette Free Gift Promotion Offer. We will send you the specified gift.

FREE GIFT CERTIFICATE

ITEM	A. GOLD TONE EARRINGS	B. GOLD TONE BRACELET	C. GOLD TONE NECKLACE
# of proofs-of-purchase required	3	6	9
Postage and Handling	$1.75	$2.25	$2.75
Check one	☐	☐	☐

Name: _____

Address: _____

City: _____ State: _____ Zip Code: _____

Mail this certificate, specified number of proofs-of-purchase and a check or money order for postage and handling to: HARLEQUIN/SILHOUETTE FREE GIFT OFFER 1992, P.O. Box 9057, Buffalo, NY 14269-9057. Requests must be received by July 31, 1992.

PLUS—Every time you submit a completed certificate with the correct number of proofs-of-purchase, you are automatically entered in our MILLION DOLLAR SWEEPSTAKES! No purchase or obligation necessary to enter. See below for alternate means of entry and how to obtain complete sweepstakes rules.

MILLION DOLLAR SWEEPSTAKES
NO PURCHASE OR OBLIGATION NECESSARY TO ENTER

To enter, hand-print (mechanical reproductions are not acceptable) your name and address on a 3″ × 5″ card and mail to Million Dollar Sweepstakes 6097, c/o either P.O. Box 9056, Buffalo, NY 14269-9056 or P.O. Box 621, Fort Erie, Ontario L2A 5X3. Limit: one entry per envelope. Entries must be sent via 1st-class mail. For eligibility, entries must be received no later than March 31, 1994. No liability is assumed for printing errors, lost, late or misdirected entries.

Sweepstakes is open to persons 18 years of age or older. All applicable laws and regulations apply. Sweepstakes offer void wherever prohibited by law. Prizewinners will be determined no later than May 1994. Chances of winning are determined by the number of entries distributed and received. For a copy of the Official Rules governing this sweepstakes offer, send a self-addressed, stamped envelope (WA residents need not affix return postage) to: Million Dollar Sweepstakes Rules, P.O. Box 4733, Blair, NE 68009.

✂ HT2U

ONE PROOF-OF-PURCHASE

To collect your fabulous FREE GIFT you must include the necessary FREE GIFT proofs-of-purchase with a properly completed offer certificate.

(See inside back cover for offer details)